ALSO BY STACY DeKEYSER

Jump the Cracks

THE BRIXEN WITCH

STACY DEKEYSER

MARGARET K. McELDERRY BOOKS
New York   London   Toronto   Sydney   New Delhi

MARGARET K. McELDERRY BOOKS
An imprint of Simon & Schuster Children's Publishing Division
1230 Avenue of the Americas, New York, New York 10020

This book is a work of fiction. Any references to historical events, real people, or real places are used fictitiously. Other names, characters, places, and events are products of the author's imagination, and any resemblance to actual events or places or persons, living or dead, is entirely coincidental.

MARGARET K. McELDERRY BOOKS is a trademark of Simon & Schuster, Inc.
For information about special discounts for bulk purchases, please contact Simon & Schuster Special Sales at 1-866-506-1949 or business@simonandschuster.com.
The Simon & Schuster Speakers Bureau can bring authors to your live event. For more information or to book an event, contact the Simon & Schuster Speakers Bureau at 1-866-248-3049 or visit our website at www.simonspeakers.com.
Also available in a Margaret K. McElderry Books hardcover edition
Book design by Debra Sfetsios-Conover
The text for this book is set in Cochin.
The illustrations for this book are rendered in Illustrator.
Manufactured in the United States of America
0513 OFF
First Margaret K. McElderry Books paperback edition June 2013
10 9 8 7 6 5 4 3 2 1
The Library of Congress has cataloged the hardcover edition as follows:
DeKeyser, Stacy.
The Brixen Witch / Stacy DeKeyser. — 1st ed.
p. cm.
Summary: Twelve-year-old Rudi stumbles upon a witch's lair while out hunting, takes a gold coin he finds there but loses it again, then must deal with the witch's servant who promises to end the town's rat infestation only if he receives that gold coin, in a story reminiscent of The Pied Piper of Hamelin.
ISBN 978-1-4424-3328-1 (hardcover)
ISBN 978-1-4424-3330-4 (eBook)
[1. Witchcraft — Fiction. 2. Community life — Fiction. 3. Rats — Fiction. 4. Magic — Fiction.] I. Title.
PZ7.D3682Bri 2012
[Fic] — dc23
2011033680
ISBN 978-1-4424-3329-8 (pbk)

FOR STEPHANIE

ACKNOWLEDGMENTS

I am grateful to an entire community of book lovers, especially these in particular, who helped this book come into the world:

To my first readers, Dori Chaconas, Kim Marcus, Audrey Vernick, and the Tuesday Writers of West Hartford, Connecticut, for their honest feedback, steadfast friendship, and positive vibes.

To the Connecticut Commission on Culture and Tourism, for its generous Artist Fellowship.

To Tracey Adams and everyone at Adams Literary, for their passion, energy, and unwavering faith.

To everyone at Margaret K. McElderry Books, especially Karen Wojtyla, who has been exactly the right midwife for this book. Her enthusiasm, thoughtfulness, and deft touch have reminded me at every step how lucky I am to be part of MKM's literary legacy.

To all my family for their support, especially Kelly, Tom, and Steven, whose love, good humor, and patience allow me to do what I do.

CHAPTER I

RUDI BAUER ran for his life and cursed his bad luck. He would never have touched the gold coin—much less put it in his pocket—if he'd known it belonged to a witch.

It had been a blustery morning, with more than a hint of snow stinging his nostrils, when Rudi left his warm cottage and climbed the high meadow to hunt rabbits in the shadow of the Berg. All day long he scrambled on the mountain, but his aim was crooked, or perhaps it was his slingshot. By dusk, icy pellets stabbed Rudi's hands and face, and he had nothing to show for the day but the golden guilder in his pocket and its rightful owner flinging hexes down the mountain in his wake.

So now here he was, half running, half stumbling downslope, the wind and sleet screaming in his ears.

Or was it the witch?

Rudi didn't stop to find out. He hurtled down the mountain, his legs threatening to give way and send him off the edge and onto the rocks below.

But he wasn't thinking of that. Or he was trying not to. He was thinking how remarkable it was that the witch was real after all. All this time, he'd assumed she was nothing but a fairy tale; a bedtime fable told to every child in the village of Brixen. His own mother had often told him the story of the Brixen Witch, who lived under the mountain, hidden and silent so long as no one disturbed her domain.

He had never liked that story at bedtime. It did not result in happy dreams.

And other than a few stories, nothing much was said about the witch in Brixen. People said it was bad luck to talk of such things.

"So I found the entrance to her lair," thought Rudi to himself as darkness fell and the lights of the village appeared below through the slanting pellets of ice. "I wonder if anyone else knows where it is. I wonder if I'd ever be able to find it again."

But he couldn't imagine ever wanting to find it again. Every blink of his eyes brought a flash of memory: the gaping mouth; the teeth like spikes; the foul icy breath. And the screech—it had been painful to his ears, like a thousand cats fighting in a room with walls of stone.

Rudi shuddered as he hurled himself toward his own front door. One last look over his shoulder. One last ear-piercing shriek that may have been the storm, but may have been—

And he crashed into the house, somersaulting onto the floor as the door hit the wall with a bang. In one quick instant he was surrounded by everyone he loved most dearly in the world, and he had never been happier to see them.

"Close the door, boy!" yelled his father, jumping from his chair and spilling his pipe onto Rudi's head. "You're letting October into the house!"

"By the saints!" said his mother. "You're muddy as a salamander. And now look at my rug."

"Where are the rabbits?" said Oma. "I'm getting too old to eat my dinner so late."

Rudi blinked up at them, trying to catch his breath. He swallowed hard, lifted his head, and croaked, "Witch." Then he collapsed into a heap.

"Which what?" said Oma, *tsk*ing and nudging Rudi with her toe. "The boy needs to learn to speak up. I don't see any rabbits on his belt."

"Nor do I," said his mother, sighing. "Then it's barley soup again."

Rudi sat up, dug pipe ash out of his ear, and tried to speak calmly. But all he could manage was, "A cave . . . on the mountain . . . something chased me. . . ."

3

"What was it?" said his father. "A bear? A wolf?" He squinted at Rudi. "A bad-tempered marmot?"

"Should have shot it anyway," said Oma. "It would have been as tasty as rabbit, I'm sure." She smacked her gums.

Rudi regarded his slingshot and his grandmother in turn. "It was bigger than me," he told her. "With teeth. And claws. And a screech like the Devil himself."

"Rudolf Augustin Bauer!" scolded his mother. "Such stories you tell!"

Rudi considered that the stories he told were only those she'd told him first, but he kept silent in that regard.

Rudi's father refilled the bowl of his pipe and struck a match. "Your eyes were playing tricks on you, son. You know better than to be caught up there as the light wanes, especially when a storm threatens. Are you sure you didn't come upon a fox sleeping in its den? That would raise a snarl, I've no doubt." And he snorted and clapped Rudi on the back, so that Rudi nearly collapsed again onto the rug.

Rudi sighed. His father must be right. It had been getting dark, and the snow had started to fly, and it had become difficult to see. He smiled crookedly, and felt his face grow warm, and scratched the back of his head.

"You're right, Papa," he said. "That was it. I'm sure it was a fox." And Rudi stood on the rug, kicked off his muddy boots (to his mother's exasperation), and took himself up the stairs to clean up.

But as he pulled off his grass-stained trousers, a new thought popped into his head. He plunged his hand deep into his pocket, and his fingers closed around something hard and flat and round.

A golden guilder.

It gleamed softly, even in the dimness of the loft, and it was unlike anything he'd ever seen. Not that he'd often seen any gold coin up close before. But it had a thickness about it, and markings he couldn't read.

"What kind of fox keeps an old gold coin in its den?" he whispered to himself. But he decided it was just coincidence. If Rudi had stumbled upon the cave, why not someone else? Another hunter had dropped the coin long ago, and today Rudi had found it. That was all.

His mind wandered to what he might be able to buy with such a coin. A new pair of skis? A new rug for his mother? A slingshot that actually worked?

And then one ragged syllable burst from Oma's mouth, flew up the stairs, and scraped Rudi's eardrums.

"Witch!"

5

Rudi's breath stopped in his throat. The coin fell from his hand onto his stockinged foot and rolled under his bed. He stifled a curse.

"Which what?" boomed Papa's voice from below. Then he laughed. "Is that how you play the game, Mother?"

Rudi scrambled into clean trousers, fumbled beneath the bed for the coin, and jammed it under his pillow. "How's that, Oma?" he called over the railing, his voice cracking.

"When you first spilled into the house all breathless and red in the face," she called up to him, "you said 'witch.' Didn't you?" Oma's mind was sharp. It was her ears that sometimes lagged behind, but they always caught up eventually, and that's what they were doing now.

Rudi gulped, and resisted the urge to glance back at his pillow. "I was being silly," he called down. "Like Papa said—it was a trick of the light."

Oma squinted up at him for a moment. Then she shrugged and sat herself down to dinner. "As you say. You were there, not I."

Rudi breathed a sigh of relief, which brought the aroma of hot barley soup and fried apples to his nostrils. He bounded down the stairs, his appetite surging.

"All I mean to say," said Oma, as if the conversation had not just ended, "is that if you did visit a witch, I hope you didn't take anything. Anyone who steals from the Brixen Witch's hoard is hounded without mercy until she gets her treasure back. That's all I mean to say."

And Oma dipped her spoon into her bowl and slurped her soup.

CHAPTER 2

RUDI COULD not sleep.

He blamed the storm, which continued into the night without relief. The wind rattled the shutters, and it made an eerie noise that sounded to Rudi's ears like some kind of tuneless singing, or the distant playing of a pennywhistle. In their own corners of the loft, his family somehow managed to sleep undisturbed.

Rudi dragged his pillow over his head, and his cheek came to rest on a spot of cool metal. The golden guilder. The cursed coin. Oma's words pushed themselves at him again, as they had done all that evening, no matter how he'd tried to keep them away. And if that weren't enough, it seemed to Rudi that the pillow did nothing to muffle the tuneless song.

He sat up and scanned the darkness. Then he slid out of bed and stepped to his trunk, not bothering to tread softly. The noise of the storm stifled all other sound, even Oma's snores. Rudi buried the coin deep within the folds of his summerweight woolens, dropped the lid of his trunk, and scuttled back to bed.

At that moment the wind gave a frightful howl. It wrenched a shutter free from its latch and banged it against the house. The panes of the window rattled as the sleet battered the glass like handfuls of stones. For the briefest instant, Rudi thought he glimpsed a flash of color through the window— red, and then yellow—and then he saw something else just beyond the glass.

A face?

"Brrrf!" came a groggy deep voice from the other end of the loft. "What the—*grmph*—shutter!" And Papa tumbled out of bed and lurched half-asleep toward the window. Rudi was sure that the face outside the window was only a result of his own terrified imagination, but just in case, he jumped out of bed and grabbed the hem of Papa's nightshirt.

Papa swung the windowpane inward, reached out into the storm, gasped *"buh!"* as he was splashed with sleet, grabbed the shutter, pulled it tight, and hooked the latch. Then he shut the window again and turned back toward the room, now fully awake and blinking away ice pellets.

"What?—" Papa said, nearly stepping on Rudi. "Why didn't you get the shutter if you were up? And why is there still a draft in here?" Papa's gaze fell upon Rudi's hand, which was still holding his father's nightshirt and revealing a good bit of beefy bare leg.

Papa tugged his shirt out of Rudi's grasp, and a laugh burst from his lips. "Twelve years old and still afraid of a storm, eh, boy?" He tousled Rudi's hair. "I won't tell. It's a night for the Devil himself out there, don't tell your mother I said that." A shiver ran its course from Papa's knees to his shoulders, and for a moment Rudi wondered if the source of the shiver was the storm, the Devil, or his mother. Papa shuffled back to bed, leaving Rudi to stand on the cold floor with his mouth hanging open.

Now it was Rudi who blinked. What had he seen outside the window? It must have been an illusion, created by the slashing sleet against the panes. He recalled how the wavy glass shone with rainbow colors during summer rainstorms, when sunlight peeked from behind the clouds and struck the window at just the right angle. Yes, that's what had happened now. Something like that.

Proud of himself for thinking so logically despite

the disturbances of the night, Rudi clambered into bed for a second time. He turned over and tried to sleep.

It was no use. He couldn't shake the tuneless song from his head, even though he knew it was just the wind twisting itself through the chinks in the walls and into his ears. He concentrated on hearing only the wind, and blocking from his mind whatever musical sound he thought he heard entwined with the sound of the storm.

But he could not. If anything, Rudi heard the tune even more loudly than before.

And now he heard a scratching at the window.

It was only a pinecone, Rudi told himself. Or a bit of branch that had caught in the shutter, and now it was rubbing against the windowpane. Rudi would not prove his father right about being frightened of a storm. He sat up in bed, intending to scold himself, but instead of whispering "Stop it, Rudi!" different words spilled from his mouth:

"Go away!"

But the scratching continued, and the shutter rattled (though this time it did not give way), and now Rudi was certain that the music—the tuneless song that sounded something like the wail of a pennywhistle—was not the wind, and it was not his imagination.

He slid under his blankets until they covered his

head, and he did not sleep, but could only wait for morning.

Rudi sat up with a start. He must have dozed after all, because now he heard a different sound outside the window. The sound of the wind not blowing.

No sleet lashed against the house. Nothing rattled the windows. The storm had passed.

So why did that maddening tune still prickle his ears?

It was not yet first light, but Rudi rolled out of bed and stumbled down the stairs to clear his head.

"So," came a familiar voice from somewhere in the room.

"Oma?" Rudi rubbed his eyes and strained to see in the dark. "You're up already?"

"Of course I'm up," she said. "It's morning, isn't it? Besides, I couldn't sleep with that infernal noise."

"Noise?" Rudi squeaked, and he glanced over his shoulder and up the stairs.

"Did you miss the whole storm, child? By the saints, you're a sound sleeper."

"Oh, that," Rudi said weakly, and he recalled how he hadn't heard her usual snoring. He wondered how much of the night's activity she might have heard or seen for herself. He stirred the embers in the hearth until a small tongue of flame awoke.

"Truthfully, Oma, I did not sleep well either," confided Rudi, though he hadn't planned on saying it. But it seemed that Oma . . . knew things. He decided to venture a conversation. "Have you ever gotten a tune stuck in your head?"

Oma nodded, which started her chair to rocking. "It happens every time I hear little girls skipping rope in the lane," she said. "It's a sprightly melody they sing, but after a few minutes I'm ready to scrape a spoon across slate just to chase it out of my head." She rocked, and joints creaked. Rudi wondered if the creaking joints belonged to the chair or to Oma. Perhaps to both.

He added kindling to the fire. "I've seen you chase away the little girls instead."

Oma winked at him. "Oh, they always come back. Those girls are sweet on you, especially that tanner's daughter. You brought out water and a plate of tarts for them once, and now we'll never be rid of them."

Rudi's face burned, and it wasn't from the heat of the fire. "They were thirsty. I couldn't let a troop of silly little girls go thirsty."

"Certainly not," said Oma. "Funny you should

ask about sticky tunes. It's been many a long year, but once or twice in my life I've heard the witch's tune."

Rudi let out a breath. He hadn't realized he'd been holding it.

"I heard it again last night," said Oma, studying his face. "And I can hear it now."

Rudi gaped at her. For a fleeting moment he was relieved to know the music wasn't a phantom in his head. But just as quickly, a more foreboding thought crowded in.

It must be the coin.

"Do you mean to say—"

"I don't see how," said his grandmother, still rocking and creaking. "You took nothing from the witch's lair. Did you?" Her gaze was steady.

Rudi said nothing. Didn't Oma know it was bad luck to talk of such things?

"But I must say, that tune I hear can be nothing else. I'd know it anywhere. And no good can come of it, I'll tell you that right now. It's a good thing you didn't take anything from up on that mountain. But someone did. Someone nearby. You see, the witch enchants her treasure so that it sings to her. A tune so maddening that any fool who steals even the smallest trinket would rather return it than endure its torment. And believe me, child, the Brixen Witch will not rest until a possession of hers is returned. Trouble such as that you do not want."

Rudi swallowed hard, and into his mind's eye popped the images of the night. The flash of color, and the face in the window. "Oma, have you ever . . . seen the witch?"

"Me?" She gave a little *hmpf*. "There's very few have actually seen the witch. She prefers not to show herself."

Rudi sighed. Perhaps what he had seen last night was his imagination after all. A figment caused by the storm.

Then Oma shook a finger at him, and the fire flared on the hearth. "But I've seen her messenger. And by the saints, to this day I wish I'd seen the Devil instead. That thing you did not take? Get rid of it. Carry it back up the mountain and leave it there. Do it today. Better yet, do it now. The weather is turning, and once the snows begin, no one will be venturing up that mountain until spring. You don't want to be haunted every night from now until spring, do you?"

CHAPTER 3

THE STORM had left a clear, cold sky and a layer of ice that shimmered in the waning moonlight. In an hour's time the autumn sun would rise above the peaks, chase the shadows from the valley, and melt the ice.

But Rudi had not even an hour to waste. Oma had been right: The weather was turning. October in the mountains meant that autumn could become winter in a single shuddering breath. No traveler wanted to be caught on the Berg when that happened.

Oma had nearly pushed Rudi out of the cottage. He'd barely had time to pull on coat and boots. The golden guilder had hummed as if alive when he pulled it from the depths of his trunk, so loudly that Rudi had feared it would wake his parents.

"Remember," Oma whispered, "take it high

enough so that you're out of sight of the village. Leave it where the witch's servant can find it, but away from the trodden paths. You don't want some other poor fool to stumble upon it and start the trouble all over again."

Rudi nodded and jammed the coin deep into his pocket. "I promise," he told her. "I'll tell you all about it when I get back."

She shook her head. "It's bad luck to talk of such things."

Oma handed Rudi his walking stick. She tugged his collar tighter around his neck, looked him up and down, and then patted his cheek. "I'll tell your mother you've gone fishing." And she nudged him out the door with more strength than an old woman ought to have.

Rudi wished he could have stayed indoors until proper morning came. But in a moment's time he was glad to be the only one up and about. With every tick of the steeple clock the enchanted tune grew louder. Soon there would be no denying the awkward truth to anyone within earshot: His pants were singing.

Rudi stepped with care, for every surface was encrusted with ice. He grasped the railing of the footbridge and pulled himself across. If he slipped into the frigid river Brix below, his journey would be finished before it had begun.

Cursing under his breath, Rudi skidded off the bridge and skated along the path. The coin continued to wail, so that Rudi feared the noise would spook the sure-footed cows that now lumbered up the hill to graze in the near meadow.

Once he reached the forest, the walking was easier, for the sleet had not much penetrated the canopy of pines. But Rudi knew that the high meadow would be treacherous. He was glad to have his walking stick.

Rudi shivered as he emerged from the woods. The sun was higher now, and the glaciers that clung to the western peaks shimmered, nearly blinding him. The Berg was the highest of those peaks, but it did not shimmer. Hewn from sharp black rock, the Berg swallowed whatever light tried to touch it. No trees grew on it. Snow would not cling to its slopes. Only the uppermost summit ever saw sunlight, surrounded as it was by the other mountains. The witch lived in the Berg for that reason, or so said the legends. She preferred the darkness, and the cold, and the solitude.

But the sunlight had not yet reached the bottom of the valley, and that was why Rudi shivered. The tune in his pocket had been growing ever louder, so that now Rudi glanced from side to side as he walked. He imagined that at any moment, the witch's servant might fly down to smite him and grab the coin.

Rudi looked around. The path had emerged from the forest not above the tree line but at a side clearing, at a place where the view was clear all the way down to the village. The path had been chosen long ago for just this reason: here the hunters and mountaineers of the Brixen Valley could establish their position on the landscape, and satisfy themselves that no disaster had befallen the village in their absence.

Today it only meant that Rudi had to climb higher. *High enough so that you're out of sight of the village*, Oma had said. He trudged along the path that led up and around the edge of the forest, but then he stopped. *Away from the trodden paths*, Oma had also said. Rudi surveyed his surroundings and considered his options.

The trail wound upward and meandered across the slope, then back again in a series of switchbacks. Eventually it led to the top of the tree line and onto the high meadow. Rudi imagined that it, too, had been laid out long ago, probably by cows, who by nature kept to a horizontal path whenever possible.

"Well, I'm not a cow," said Rudi to himself, because he eyed a shortcut. He wondered how he'd never noticed it before. It was a bit steeper than the worn path, but it would take him in a straight line up to the high meadow and sufficiently out of sight of the village. He was a good climber, and he had a good stick, and now the sun was high enough to melt the ice and make his going less treacherous. Besides, the singing in his pocket was grating on his nerves—like a spoon on slate, as Oma had said. He ached to be rid of the coin.

So Rudi stepped off the path and started upslope, whistling in an attempt to drown out the coin's wailing and calm his own jangled nerves.

But the slope was steeper than it had appeared from the bottom. Before long, Rudi's breathing became labored, and his legs grew wobbly, and he seemed to be not a single step closer to the edge of the meadow above. With each step the ground became looser and more rocky, and soon there was no soil to speak of at all, but only scree—piles of loose, sharp rock that shifted under his feet.

Rudi tried to find a better route, but by now he was entirely surrounded by the scree. Even going back the way he'd come would be tricky. If he slipped now, there would be nothing to break his fall except the trees far below. He had no choice but to keep climbing.

The coin sang louder. Rudi scrambled and stumbled. If the witch's servant found him now and truly did want to smite him, there would be no escape, and he'd have no defense.

Such a thought caused Rudi's heart to pound in his chest and his breath to catch in his throat. His hands became moist with sweat, so that he could barely grasp his walking stick.

Then Rudi slipped. His stick caught at a bad angle and broke in two, the bottom half skidding away down the mountain. Rudi caught himself with his free hand and one knee, which both pounded onto sharp rock. He groaned in pain, and as his ears filled with the sound of his own voice, they heard something else. It might have been the wind. But it sounded like laughter. Wispy, malevolent laughter.

The blood would have frozen in Rudi's veins, if such a thing were truly possible. He scrambled to his feet as best he could and brandished the stump of his walking stick.

The laughter grew louder, and it seemed to come from all directions, so that Rudi had no idea which way to turn. One twist of his body and he'd lose his footing again, and that would more than likely be the end of him. He'd career down the scree, all the way to the forest clearing, and quite likely the loose rock would follow him in an avalanche and bury him forever.

In a surge of dread and panic, Rudi reached into his pocket and his fingers hunted for the golden guilder. "Curse the witch and her servant," he thought. "Let them have their precious coin."

21

But Rudi could not draw out the coin. It was tangled in the folds of his pocket, as if refusing to come out into daylight.

Then Rudi slipped again. He started to slide, and he gained speed, and he rattled down the mountain in a hailstorm of rock and gravel, the cursed golden guilder still in his pocket.

To his surprise, he did not feel pain, though his body scraped and bounced along the scree. He felt only a desperate fear of being buried with the coin. Finally, he managed to yank the guilder from his pocket. The trees loomed up at him from below, growing nearer and larger with every heartbeat.

Just before the trees interrupted his slide, Rudi let go of the coin.

And that night, after Rudi had managed to drag himself home, scraped and bruised and shaken, snow fell on the mountain, heavy and deep and silent.

CHAPTER 4

RUDI WOKE with a gasp. Clutching his blankets under his chin, he dared to steal a peek at the window.

There was nothing there but the pale gray light of an April dawn.

He fell back onto his pillow and closed his eyes, forcing himself to take three slow, deep breaths, in an effort to ease the pounding in his chest.

This had become a daily ritual for Rudi.

But he had only counted to two when a sound intruded, and set Rudi's heart thumping once more.

"Pssssht!"

Rudi lay very still. He held his breath and half opened one eye. A huge moony face loomed just inches from his own.

"Oma?"

"You're talking in your sleep again," she hissed. "I can hear you all the way into the far corner of the loft."

Rudi gulped. "You can? What did I say? And what do you mean, *again*?"

Oma sniffed. "You know what I mean. Come downstairs and make us some tea."

Rudi followed obediently, casting one last look toward the window. Once they were down the stairs and the kettle was on the fire, Oma motioned for him to sit down.

"Do you know what I saw yesterday on the riverbank?" she said, scooting her chair closer to the grate.

Rudi was too tired to venture a guess, but Oma didn't wait for an answer.

"I saw a purple crocus pushing up through a patch of snow." She poked his shoulder. "The first blossom of spring."

Rudi yawned. "That's nice, Oma. Why are you telling me this?"

"Because here it is springtime, and you've been thrashing about in your bed nearly every night since the first winter storm," she told him. "It's a good thing your parents sleep like rocks. They'd think you more than half mad, the way you carry on."

Rudi cleared his throat. "How do I carry on, exactly?"

Oma rocked in her chair and studied the rafters. "Let's see . . . you mutter such things as *Go away* and *No no no* and *Take it!* Sometimes you mumble on about witches and smiting and such . . . and sometimes you just say *Ah-yeeeeeeeee!*"

"Oh," said Rudi in a small voice. He reached for the steaming kettle, hoping that its weight would still the tremor in his hands. "I'll make the tea."

Oma cocked her head in the direction of the Berg. "Wasn't it just before the first snows of winter that you went on your . . . excursion?"

Rudi pretended to think about it, but then he sighed and nodded.

Oma nodded too. "So. Winter has come and gone, and here it is springtime. I think you'd better tell me what happened on the mountain that day."

Rudi shook his head. "It's bad luck to talk of such things. You said so."

"I'd say your luck is already bad," said Oma. "Perhaps it's time you sought the counsel of someone older and wiser than yourself. Someone with experience and knowledge of such things as witches."

"Do you know someone like that?" said Rudi hopefully.

Oma tapped him on the head. "Is it your luck that's bad, or just your sense? I'm talking about my own self here."

A familiar prickly notion tickled the edges of Rudi's mind: Whether she wanted to talk about it or not, Oma *knew* things.

Now she squinted at him. "A person doesn't live in Brixen for seventy-some years without learning a thing or two about this and that. You learn where the elderberries grow fattest, and when to pick them. You come to know each cow by the feel of her udder. And sooner or later, you're bound to cross paths with the witch."

Rudi stared at his grandmother. "Do you mean—"

"Then there is her servant," Oma continued. "He's been known to show his face in Brixen from time to time."

"His face?" Rudi gulped. "What does the witch's servant look like?"

"I haven't seen him for many a long year, thank the saints for small blessings. But such a sight I could never forget. Beneath his cloak he wears a patchwork shirt, stitched together from scraps left behind by the poor souls who wander too far up the mountain, catching their clothing on the rocks. His hair is like a thistle burr. His teeth are sharp as saw blades, and his eyes are black as a moonless night. The cold of the Berg is always upon him. His touch is like ice, and simply walking near him sends a chill through your body."

Rudi shivered.

Oma shook a finger at him. "Precisely. Now then, perhaps you'd better tell me your story. But first, where is that tea you promised me? I'm parched."

Rudi poured the boiling water into the teapot with leaves of dried chamomile and nettle. Then he told Oma everything that had happened on the mountain that day, when he'd tried to return the coin but lost it instead. "The coin was well and truly buried. I could no longer hear it singing, and so I supposed no one else could either. Though truthfully, I didn't stay to listen. It was such a relief to be rid of it."

Oma rocked and nodded. "And how long did that relief last?"

Rudi groaned. "There has been only torment ever since. Every day I feel something watching me. Every night I dream of a face in the window, and it's the face you described. The witch's servant. He has followed me here. He wants his coin, but I don't have it anymore. It's lost."

The fire crackled in the grate and cast long shadows across Oma's wrinkled face. She rocked forward in her chair and warmed her hands. "Do you know where the coin is buried, more or less?"

"More or less," answered Rudi.

"Then it's not lost, strictly speaking. And it's not *his* coin. It belongs to the Brixen Witch. So long as that coin is unaccounted for, your nights will be sleepless." She filled two mugs with tea and handed one to Rudi. "You still have a problem. But you can solve it once the mountain paths are clear of snow."

Rudi nodded eagerly. "How much longer before the paths are clear, do you think?" He gulped his tea in an effort to calm his queasy stomach, but he only managed to scald his throat.

"The animals are always the first to know. When goats from Klausen wander down from the high meadow looking for spring grass, you'll know the way is passable." Oma sipped her tea and rocked in her chair. "Goat bells. Listen for the goat bells."

CHAPTER 5

AND SO THE crocuses bloomed in Brixen, and then the Lenten roses. Day by day the sun reached higher in the sky, and little by little the snows melted. Meanwhile, Rudi carved a new walking stick, and he tended his father's cows, and he peered up toward the high meadow, waiting for the day he could climb the Berg and release himself from torment.

For his torment continued, especially at night, when he had nothing to keep himself busy. If his nights weren't altogether sleepless, they were fitful and restless, and full of odd dreams.

Then, early one morning, when the valley was awash in fragrant greens and yellows and pinks, Rudi awoke to the sound of goat bells.

He sprang out of bed, every muscle surging with

an energy he had not felt in months. He marveled at how lively he felt, simply from the thought of finding the coin and being rid of the curse.

But then Rudi stopped, and he realized another reason for his vigor.

For the first time since October, he had slept soundly all night.

There must be a simple reason, Rudi told himself. Perhaps he had finally learned to ignore the prickly feeling that he was being watched. Perhaps the hard work that came with the spring—the milking, and the cheese making, and clearing of the land for sowing—brought such a pleasant exhaustion that even nightmares could not penetrate it. Perhaps the witch's servant had been listening for goat bells too. Perhaps, at last, he recovered the infernal treasure from beneath the rubble on the mountain, and had returned it to its owner in her dim and dreary cave.

Or perhaps by now the witch had simply given up.

"She will never give up," remarked Oma. "The witch must have found the coin herself—or her servant did. At any rate, it seems she has her treasure back. That can be the only reason your nightmares have stopped."

The reason did not much matter to Rudi. He felt only relief and peace. Finally, he could enjoy the blessed pleasure of his daily life.

Rudi loved working on his father's farm. He loved the smell of the thawing earth, the sprouting grass, and the newborn calves. He loved the squish of mud under his boots, and the warm sun on his neck, and the sound of his mother's voice calling him to dinner as the light faded and cast the shadow of the Berg upon the farm.

And in the warm evenings, Rudi loved to wander with his family toward the village square to join the nightly gathering. Here was where the townspeople of Brixen exchanged news, shared a bit of tobacco, and watched the children grow.

This night was no different, and for that, Rudi was happily grateful.

The miller's newborn son was to be named Steffan, and he would be christened in two weeks' time. Mama chimed in with the other matrons, offering to weave white ribbons to decorate the church.

Old Mistress Gerta had not risen from bed in a week, and her daughter—Not-So-Old Mistress Gerta—fretted that the next time the sun shone down upon her mother, it would be while being carried to the churchyard. Oma promised to visit in the morning and talk some sense into the old woman. Rudi knew that if any life remained in Old Mistress Gerta, she'd use it to get out of bed and venture outdoors just to escape Oma's pestering.

Which, he supposed, was the whole point.

The price of coal had gone up again, as had the price of beer. What was the world coming to, Papa complained, if even the brewer-monks at the Abbey of St. Adolphus tried to wring the townspeople dry? Otto the baker pointed out that the monks must pay more for their coal as well, and so of course they must charge more for their beer. As night follows day. Papa grumbled and chewed on the stem of his pipe.

Rudi followed only bits and pieces of each conversation. They all took place at the same time, as the villagers of Brixen perched on the benches and strolled the cobbles of the town square. Meanwhile, children of all sizes yelled and chased and scurried everywhere: between the benches, around the old ladies, along the top of the churchyard wall. No one took much notice, except for the occasional distracted scolding when things got too boisterous. At such times, the nearest adult would scold whatever child needed it, and that child would obey until he was out of earshot, at which point the next adult would assume the watchful duties. No one paid attention to whose child was whose. Every child was a child of Brixen, and that was enough.

Rudi sought out the far corner of the fountain, where the boys always gathered to trade rocks from their collections, or to thumb-wrestle, or to brag of accomplishments real and imagined.

"The lynx was *this big*," declared Nicolas, spreading his arms wide. "It hissed at me, but I chased it from the chicken coop."

Konrad snorted. "My grandfather says no one's seen a lynx near Brixen since he was our age. Are you sure it wasn't a barn cat?"

At this the boys tumbled over each other in laughter—all but Nicolas, who turned red in the face. Upon noticing Rudi, he changed the subject. "Are you coming with us tonight to Johanna's house? We're going to compliment her mother's strudel, but really it's so Konrad can show Johanna his muscles. Such as they are."

Now it was Konrad's turn to blush red, and Rudi laughed along with the rest of them, relieved and thankful that life had returned to the way it should be.

And so it continued until dusk, when the smallest children were carried home on their fathers' shoulders or in their mothers' arms. The middle-size children escorted their grandparents, slowing their pace to match that of their elders. The ones nearly grown, if they had not found someone's hand to hold, hung back in bunches to snicker in envy at the hand holders. Husbands and wives strolled with their arms entwined. And so tonight, like every warm night of spring, the village of Brixen went home to bed.

But something about this night was different after all.

As dusk fell and the first lanterns were placed in windows, a scream rose from somewhere in the square.

The villagers stopped as one, and turned, straining to see who had made the noise, and why.

"Susanna Louisa, what's wrong?" said her mother.

"I saw something!" said Susanna Louisa, the tanner's daughter. She was eight years old and a skittish child, but Rudi liked her.

"Your eyes are working, then," said her father, and he scooped her up, but Susanna Louisa twisted herself in his arms and pointed toward the cobblestones.

"There!" she squealed.

Rudi squinted in the direction the girl was pointing, but he saw only shadows. He strained harder and waited to see if any of the shadows moved.

One did.

"It's just a rat," declared Nicolas. "Do you want me to catch it?"

"Is it *this big*?" asked Konrad. He spread his arms wide, and dodged the flying fist of Nicolas just in time.

"I don't like rats," Rudi heard Susanna Louisa saying as her father carted her homeward.

"No one does, my little blossom," sang her father. "They won't bother you if you don't bother them."

Nervous and relieved laughter filtered through the night air as the villagers dispersed into the lanes and alleys surrounding the square.

But from somewhere behind him, Rudi overheard one of his neighbors.

"Won't bother you, eh?" muttered the man to his companion. "Perhaps not, but I don't like it. 'Tis bad luck to see a rat in the shadow of the churchyard wall. Mark my words, nothing good can come of that."

At these words, Rudi felt a familiar, prickly feeling. What did it mean?

Then a hand grabbed his elbow. He started, but only for a moment. The hand was Oma's.

"Pay no attention to that fool," she said as they shuffled home together. "Sometimes a rat is just a rat."

CHAPTER 6

IT WAS A hot midafternoon in June. Rudi and Papa had come indoors for lunch, and they stayed in for a bit of a snooze in the cool, dark cottage.

Just as Papa's snores filled the house, something banged on the door, startling Rudi awake. He shook the grogginess from his head and opened the door, squinting in the bright sunlight.

Susanna Louisa, the tanner's sweet little skittish child, was bouncing on the doorstep.

"You knock loudly for such a mite of a girl," Rudi said without further greeting.

In answer, Susanna Louisa held up a stone that was as big as her fist.

"Ah," said Rudi. "No wonder. Why did you knock with the stone?"

"So someone would open your door. People can

always hear me better when I knock with a stone."

Rudi stifled a smile and shaded his eyes with his hand. "It worked. Now what?"

Susanna Louisa blinked, and then she stood up straight and cleared her throat, as if just now remembering the purpose of her visit. "Mama says can we borrow your cat."

Rudi shook his head. "We haven't got a cat."

"Yes you do," said Susanna Louisa. "I've seen it in your barn. The gray and white stripey one."

"Zick-Zack? She's not ours, really. More like she belongs to herself."

"Even so," said the girl. "I need her."

"Then go catch her," said Rudi.

"I can't. She's too fast. And she scratches."

"Then I suppose you can't have her, can you?" And Rudi yawned and turned, ready to close the door.

"Wait!" cried Susanna Louisa. "Mama says we need a cat. Very badly. Can you help me find a cat?"

Rudi had the feeling he would regret asking his next question, but curiosity got the better of him. "And why do you need a cat?"

"To eat the mouses," said Susanna Louisa. "Mama says we have too many and she can't catch them all herself and Papa is no use so we need a cat." She took a breath. "A hungry cat would be best."

Rudi scratched his head. "Zick-Zack has plenty of mice to eat around the barn, so even if you could catch her, I don't think she'd be much help. What about Old Mistress Gerta? Doesn't she have a house cat? You could ask her."

Susanna Louisa shook her head. "I asked her already, but she says no. Says she's got mouses too and can't spare her cat." The little girl blinked a teary eye. "I've asked everyone. Everyone says the same thing. Everyone has mouses." She hung her head, let the stone fall from her hand, and began trudging homeward.

"Wait!" called Rudi. He pulled on his boots, closed the door behind him, and fell into step beside her in the dusty lane. "What do you mean, everyone has mice?"

Susanna Louisa shrugged. "That's what everyone says. I say we need to borrow a cat, and everyone says no, we can't spare the cat because of the mouses."

"You're sure you've asked everyone?"

Susanna Louisa nodded. "I saved you for last. Because you only have that nasty mean Zick-Zack, and I didn't want to try and catch her. But Mama is near going mad. She told me, 'Don't come home without a hungry cat in your arms, Susanna Louisa, or you'll be sleeping with mouses in your bed tonight.'" And Susanna Louisa stopped walking, stood on her tiptoes, and whispered to Rudi, "I don't want mouses in my bed."

Rudi stopped too. The little girl looked so forlorn and worried that his heart melted.

"What if I help you catch the mice?"

"You?" said Susanna Louisa, and her face brightened. "Do you know how?"

"Well . . . ," said Rudi, not quite ready to admit his shortcomings to an eight-year-old, "I'm sure it can't be that hard. We'll go back to my house and get a bit of cheese. Then we'll set some traps, and *poof*! No more mice." He smiled down at Susanna Louisa, but resisted the urge to pat her on the head.

"Oh, no," said the girl solemnly. "We've tried that. For days. It does no good. It seems the more we trap, the more come out of hiding. Under the floorboards, amongst the thatch, in the wood pile. It's a regular mousie party!"

Now they had arrived at the tanner's cottage. Susanna Louisa's house.

From inside, Rudi could hear scuffling and cursing and muffled *thwack*ing. Then the door opened and two black rats scurried out, followed by a large, red-faced woman waving a broom in their wake. The rats vanished under the house, and the woman narrowly avoided smacking Rudi with the broom.

"Oh!" she exclaimed, straightening herself and tucking a lock of hair under her cap. "Good afternoon, Rudi. What brings you here this sweaty day?"

Rudi kept his eye on the mistress and her broom. "Susanna Louisa," he said quietly, "those were not mice."

But Susanna Louisa was nowhere to be seen.

Mistress Tanner shook her head. "She's gone to stand on a rock in the middle of the stream. Poor child thinks rats can't swim." And Mistress Tanner plopped down on her doorstep, rested the broom across her lap, and bit her lip.

"Mistress?" ventured Rudi. "Susanna Louisa says your . . . problem might be worse than usual?"

Mistress Tanner sighed and wiped her eyes with her apron. "It's the time of year for them, I know," she said. "What with the warm weather and the abundance of smells. Still, this is worse than anything I've ever seen. The smith next door says so too, and the miller, and the baker, and everyone. It seems the vile things are overrunning Brixen. It's not a good sign." She yelped, and reached under herself, and pulled a young rat out by its long naked tail. "See this? They're hardly afeared of humans at all." She flung the creature to the side, where it squeaked and scurried toward the woodpile.

Rudi scratched his head. "We don't have such a problem at our house."

Mistress Tanner snorted. "Just wait."

As Rudi wandered homeward, he recalled the words he'd overheard that night in the village square, weeks before: *'Tis bad luck to see a rat in the shadow of the churchyard wall . . . Nothing good can come of that.*

Rudi had feared, upon hearing those words, that the Brixen Witch had leveled a new curse upon him, and upon all his neighbors too. But he could think of no reason for it. His nightmares were gone. Certainly the witch had recovered her coin.

Besides, the villagers of Brixen were a superstitious lot. They claimed enchantment and omens with every turn of the weather and with every stillborn calf.

And yet . . .

Even if the witch had not recovered her coin after all, why would she curse the entire village?

Rudi shook himself. The infestation of rats was only a coincidence. A result of the warm weather and abundant food, and nothing more. Besides, if the rats were an enchantment, wouldn't Rudi's own house be overrun with the creatures?

He turned a corner and wandered up the lane toward home.

As he approached his own front door, he heard

a shriek coming from inside the cottage. The door flew open, and his mother ran out with a bundle in her apron. She shook it frantically, and out tumbled a large, pink-tailed rat.

Mama looked at Rudi, her eyes wide and her chest heaving. Then, without a word, she stepped back into the house and slammed the door.

Through the open window, Rudi could hear Oma somewhere inside, *tsk*ing.

And Papa was still snoring.

CHAPTER 7

MISTRESS TANNER'S words proved to be prophetic. In short order, Brixen was indeed overrun with rats. Rats in the woodpiles, rats in the thatch, rats in the stream (poor little Susanna Louisa). Rats spilling down chimneys and onto hearths, scorched tails and all.

To be sure, rats were nothing new in Brixen. Much like mosquitoes and vipers and the surly barn cat Zick-Zack, rats were vile, unwelcome, barely tolerated creatures, but they played a role in the natural order of things. They provided a home for fleas. They gave parents a reason to scold children who ventured too near to dark and unhealthy corners.

But this June, something was different.

The rats were worse than ever before. True, it

was an especially warm summer, but there had been other warm summers. The cats had done all they could and were fat to prove it, but it was not enough. The dogs chased whatever rats ventured into the open, but rats were stealthy creatures, and they easily avoided a species that excelled at napping. Traps, as Susanna Louisa had told Rudi, could catch only so many rats. And there seemed to be more every day.

Rudi began to suspect there was a curse after all. He decided to ask Oma about it.

"Enchantment?" she said, and then she hummed a bit to herself, thinking. "Are you sure you've had no more nightmares since the snows melted?"

Rudi shook his head emphatically. "I sleep like a rock every night."

"Then I still say the witch has retrieved her coin. If this is a new enchantment, it's not your doing." Oma shrugged. "Then again, sometimes a rat is just a rat. There's one way to find out."

"How?" said Rudi.

"If ordinary measures get rid of the rats, then there can be no enchantment. Yes?"

"I suppose so," said Rudi. Then he frowned. "What ordinary measures have we not already tried?"

Oma tapped her own forehead. "The mayor will know."

"He will? How will the mayor know?"

She patted Rudi on the cheek. "Because I'm going to tell him, that's how."

That very evening, Rudi overheard a conversation in the bustling village square.

"Did I not say so weeks ago?" said a familiar voice. "I told you it would come to no good. And now here we are."

It was the voice Rudi had heard that night in the spring, when the trouble with rats had first begun. Now he saw that it belonged to Marco, the village blacksmith.

Oma, who had been dozing on a bench, jerked awake at the words. She stood and addressed the blacksmith, who was more than twice her size.

"Ah, Master Smith. Did you also predict that the sun would rise this morning?"

After a few seconds looking around, the blacksmith's gaze fell upon Oma, who stood more or less as high as his rib cage.

"Good evening, Mistress Bauer. You have a bone to pick with me, do you?"

She wagged a finger at him. "It seems you've spent these last weeks using all your energy in predicting and complaining. What about a remedy? Here we are, true enough. But what we need to know is this: What's to be done about it?"

"About the rats?" said Marco. "There's nothing to be done, except wait for the winter to freeze them out. Or wait for a new sign. Whichever comes first." And with that he spun away from Oma, as if their conversation had come to an end.

But Oma seemed to think otherwise.

"Sit and wait," she said to his broad back. "I suppose you needn't worry about rats chewing through your metalworks. But how will you feel when one of your beautiful fat twin babies is bitten?" Oma folded her arms and tapped her foot, and waited.

Rudi, and all the villagers within earshot, held still and waited as well.

Marco turned toward Oma once more. His face had gone pale. He opened his mouth, but nothing came out.

"*Hmph*!" said Oma. "That's what I thought." She turned away from Marco the blacksmith.

And now the conversation had come to an end.

Oma beckoned to another man in the crowd, a wiry bald man whose mustache was as wide as his face.

"Did you hear all that, mayor?" she asked him.

"Aye, mistress, I heard," said the man. "What do you think?"

"How should I know? You're the mayor."

The mayor furrowed his brow and pulled at his

mustache. "I think tomorrow night, then?"

Oma nodded. "Tomorrow night."

And so the town meeting was called to order at sunset the following day.

Rudi and his family arrived in time to hear the mayor's gavel striking. The room was already full of people, and the debate was already under way.

"My children have been afraid to go outdoors," someone was saying. Rudi recognized the voice of Not-So-Old Mistress Gerta. "Even on the sunniest of days. Then one morning a rat fell out of the rafters, and so the children ran back outdoors. Now they play in the middle of the lane, where they can see whatever might be coming toward them. I fear that one day they'll be struck by a cart."

"Seven sacks of flour," announced Jacob the miller. "That's how many have been gnawed upon and spoiled by rats. How many more before the summer is out? Soon enough no one will have bread to eat."

Even Rudi's mother had something to say. "I keep a spotless cottage. I scrub the floors, beat the rugs, wash the linens. And yet there they are, as happy to be among us as in the barn under the manure. I don't know what's gotten into the creatures."

Several villagers responded with sympathetic murmurs and nods.

"We need Herbert Wenzel," crackled a thin voice beside Rudi. "Someone needs to go to Klausen and fetch him."

The voice was Oma's. And though Rudi himself had barely heard the words, the entire room fell silent.

"Herbert Wenzel?" said the mayor from the platform. "The rat catcher?" And then, meeting Oma's steely gaze, he cleared his throat and banged his gavel. "Of course! The rat catcher. Because this is nothing more than an ordinary, disgusting infestation of rats. Who better to deal with it than an ordinary, disgust—er, a professional rat catcher?"

Rudi glanced sidelong at Oma. The mayor was proposing exactly what she had suggested the day before: If ordinary measures got rid of the rats, then there could be no enchantment.

Not in so many words, of course. It was bad luck to talk of such things.

"A rat catcher? What would that cost?" blurted Marco the blacksmith. "A pretty penny, I've no doubt."

Oma stepped forward and narrowed her eyes at Marco. "And how are those fine children of yours, Master Smith? Healthy, I hope?"

Marco the smith gulped and said to the room at large, "I think perhaps Old Mistress Bauer is right. It's time to call in a rat catcher." And then he nodded toward Oma with recently acquired respect.

Jacob the miller spoke up again. "No one is saying it won't be costly. But it's already costing me a pretty penny. Seven sacks of flour they've ruined, and more to come, I'm sure. Might as well throw money into the river. Herbert Wenzel provides a service. He'll earn every penny we pay him."

Again the voices crowded the air, each with a different opinion.

The mayor banged his gavel, which did nothing much to calm the crowd. "We all agree this cannot continue. It's time we called in an expert."

The crowd murmured and muttered. Oma crossed her arms and chewed the inside of her cheek.

The gavel again. "Master Smith has a point as well. Does anyone know how much Herbert Wenzel's service might cost?" The mayor looked around the room.

Otto the baker climbed onto a chair. "A pretty penny is right enough. My cousin lives in Klausen. He told me once that's what Wenzel charges: a penny a rat."

"He charges by the rat?" said Marco. "In that case, I say each household should pay for the rats caught within. That's fair."

Mistress Tanner stepped out of the crowd and addressed the burly blacksmith. "And how is that fair? I live next door to you, and I happen to know that whatever rats are in *my* woodpile came from *your* woodpile."

The blacksmith drew himself up to his full height. "Is that so? I'd say it was the other way around!"

Rudi half worried, half hoped it might come to blows, though he knew it would be a lopsided fight. No one stood a chance against Mistress Tanner.

"Now see here!" The mayor pounded his gavel, his voice barely heard above the discussing and the arguing. "This problem belongs to all of Brixen. We will divide Herbert Wenzel's fee among every household. All agreed?"

"Agreed," came the answer in ragged unison from the crowd.

"Master Otto," said the mayor, "would you be willing to venture to Klausen?"

The baker nodded. "I can leave at daybreak and be back in three days' time."

"It's decided, then," announced the mayor. "Good Otto the baker will fetch Herbert Wenzel, the rat catcher of Klausen. I suggest we all start counting our pennies."

And he brought down the gavel with a *bang*.

CHAPTER 8

THREE DAYS later, Otto the baker returned home to Brixen as promised, accompanied by Herbert Wenzel, the rat catcher of Klausen.

That same morning, Oma sent Rudi up to the roof to patch any holes he might find in the thatch. But his father had performed that same task only the day before. It was possible that Papa had missed a gap or two, but Rudi suspected Oma might have another purpose for pushing him up the ladder.

Then Oma mentioned (when his mother was out of earshot) that as long as Rudi was on the roof, if he happened to see any travelers coming up the road from Klausen, he should climb down and tell her.

And so, by the time anyone else in Brixen knew of the rat catcher's arrival, Oma had already invited him in and learned the names of his ferrets (Annalesa and Beatrice), how long he'd been in the trade ("Thirty years now, and I still have all my fingers!"), and how many lumps of sugar he liked in his rosehip tea (two, thank you).

Rudi's mother set to work preparing a tray for the visitor, but she appeared to be distracted. Finally, she said, "Pardon me, Master Wenzel, but are you sure *that* needs to be in the house?" She tilted her head toward a small hutch in the corner of the room. It was made of wood and wire, and it was only partly covered by an empty burlap sack.

Herbert Wenzel nodded vigorously. "Oh yes, mistress, for certain they do. They gets terrible fretful and lonesome if they can't see me. But don't you worry. Anna and Bea are the quietest, cleanest creatures you'll ever see." And Herbert Wenzel crouched and waggled a finger between the wires of the hutch. The ferrets chortled and rubbed their faces against his finger.

Rudi knelt beside him. "Do they bite?"

"Oh, no, they never bites people," said Herbert Wenzel. "The hand that feeds them and all that. Here, see for yourself."

So Rudi slid the tip of a finger between the wires of the hutch, and the two ferrets sniffed it, and examined it, and nibbled it gently. He couldn't help but laugh.

"Rudi! Must you?" said his mother, and he wondered if she'd nearly reached her limit of tolerating small furry creatures in her house, caged or not.

"It tickles," he said. He reached in farther and rubbed the top of one soft head.

Rudi's mother sighed heavily.

"Lovely little things," said Oma, wrinkling her nose. "Now tell me, Master Wenzel, I imagine you're keeping quite busy this season, what with the overabundance of vermin hereabouts. You must be up to your earlobes and eyeballs in rats."

Upon hearing this, Rudi's mother pushed the tray into Rudi's hands and announced, "I must be off. I'm sure Old Mistress Gerta needs me. For something." And she hurried out the door, barely able to conceal a shudder.

"My daughter-in-law," said Oma. "A bit queasy when it comes to talk of unpleasant things. But she bakes a lovely elderberry tart, don't you think? It's my own recipe." She motioned for Rudi to offer the tray.

Herbert Wenzel rubbed his finger on his shirt and helped himself. "Well, mistress, I can't say as I've been busy. As a matter of fact, it's been right quiet in Klausen this summer, so I was a bit surprised when Master Otto came to inquire about my services." He popped a tart into his mouth.

Oma rocked in her chair. "You don't say? So, then, why do you suppose the little beasties have chosen to visit Brixen in such numbers?"

"Oh, that's always hard to say. Mayhaps they heard about the good cooks here in Brixen." Herbert Wenzel reached for another tart and laughed at his own joke, but Oma didn't so much as smile.

"Or"—he tried again, swallowing his bite—"mayhaps an extra litter or two came to town on the coal cart or some such . . . and you know how it is with rats." He leaned forward in his chair and lowered his voice. "They multiply like rabbits."

"Ah," said Oma. "Reasonable explanations, then." She shot Rudi a look.

Herbert Wenzel tipped his head. "If there's one thing I've learned, it's that everything has a reasonable explanation." He slurped his tea and sighed contentedly. "Unless, of course, someone's done something to vex the Brixen Witch."

Rudi gulped, but Oma scowled at him, and so he remained silent.

"Still," continued Herbert Wenzel, "in all my years at the trade, I've never seen such a thing. Rats doesn't seem to be the witch's type of doing, if you know what I mean. I've always thought her hexes were more . . . poetical. Snow in July. Two-headed calves. That sort of thing." The rat catcher leaned back and rested his hands behind his head. "No, mistress, take it from me: You've nothing here but an ordinary, disgusting infestation of rats. I'll have it cleaned up in no time."

Just then Rudi heard voices outside, and a moment later there came a knock at the door.

"We have every confidence in you," said Oma to the rat catcher. And then she turned to Rudi. "Master Otto has fetched the mayor, I suppose?"

Rudi looked out the window and nodded. "Master Smith is here as well. Shall I brew more tea?"

"They haven't come for tea," said Oma. "Open the door."

So Rudi did, and after polite introductions and curious glances at the hutch in the corner, the talk turned to the business at hand.

He'd need to size things up, of course, but Herbert Wenzel supposed he could clear the village of most every rat in ten days' time. He would set traps wherever he could, and use the ferrets everywhere else. His rate of pay was a penny a rat.

"I must say, though," added Herbert Wenzel upon seeing the beet-colored face of Marco the smith, "that most times, people thinks they have more rats than they truly has. That's just the way of people. They see one rat and right off they imagine there's twenty. So let me take a look around. I could be finished in less than a week."

"Back up a minute," said Marco. "Did you say *most* every rat? I should think at that rate of pay, you'd get rid of every one. All you need is to leave two behind, and *poof*! We're right back where we started. Don't be thinking we'll call you back time after time to do the very same job."

Herbert Wenzel the rat catcher stood up tall and lifted his chin. "I'm an honest tradesman, sir. I've been at this job for thirty years—a job very few would take on, if you don't mind my saying—so I know whereof I speaks. No one can get rid of every last rat. I wish I could give you such a promise, but it's not possible. Rats is that kind of creatures."

Otto the baker put his hand on Marco's shoulder. "In all my visits to Klausen, I've never heard a word spoken against Master Wenzel. Besides, we can deal with a few rats. It will be a relief and an improvement over what we have now."

"You don't want to solve one problem only to cause another, Master Smith," said Oma from her chair. "Get rid of every rat, and where will the fleas go? Rats are a part of life, sorry to say."

Then, as if to punctuate Oma's words, the coals settled on the fire, and a startled rat scuttled out and across the room, to the noisy consternation of the ferrets in their hutch.

Herbert Wenzel sprang to action. "Hold this, boy," he ordered Rudi, tossing him the burlap sack.

Oma (who was spry when she wanted to be) jumped out of her chair, grabbed her broom, and handed it to the rat catcher, who brought it down in the corner of the room with a *WUMP*. He held the bristles tight against the floor for a few seconds, then gave one last decisive jab.

No one dared to move.

After a few seconds, Herbert Wenzel lifted the broom tentatively. Then he motioned for Rudi, who stepped forward, holding the open sack as far away from his body as his arms could reach.

The rat catcher pulled on a pair of thick gloves, bent down, and produced the result of the battle, dangling by its tail and quite dead. He dropped it into the sack.

"I'd say we've called in the right man," announced the mayor. "Let me do the honors." And he pulled a penny from his waistcoat pocket and handed it ceremoniously to Herbert Wenzel the rat catcher.

"Why, thank you, your honor," said Herbert Wenzel with a bow. He took the sack from Rudi and tied it closed. "Well done, boy. It always makes things easier to have a helper on the job. I shares one-fifth of my earnings when I has a helper. Are you game for the task?"

Rudi's eyes grew wide. He'd never earned a real wage before.

"You ought to take that up with his father," said Oma, settling back into her chair.

Then came a cooing noise from the hutch in the corner.

"Would I be able to work with the ferrets?" asked Rudi.

"Why, of course," said the rat catcher. "That's what my little dears is for. They loves to catch rats. And I can tell they like you already."

"Your mother would not approve," warned Oma, and Rudi knew she was right.

And yet he did not stop the words from spilling out: "I'll do it."

Herbert Wenzel smiled and held his hand out to Rudi. "Congratulations, boy. It seems as if you're hired."

CHAPTER 9

AND SO THE next morning, Rudi became the rat catcher's assistant.

He learned to handle Annalesa and Beatrice, so that they quickly grew to trust him and obey the sound of his voice.

Then, beginning at Rudi's own house, Herbert Wenzel and his ferrets instructed Rudi in the rat catcher's trade.

"First we gets permission from the master and mistress, because we has to pull up some floorboards." Herbert Wenzel looked to Rudi's parents, who stood in the doorway with arms crossed and forlorn expressions on their faces.

Papa nodded solemnly. "We'll attend to the milking, then. Good luck." With that they hurried out and shut the door behind them.

Herbert Wenzel surveyed the room, and produced a crowbar from his bag. He commenced prying up two of the wide floorboards, one at either end of the room. He laid them carefully across the rug, lit a candle, and then knelt alongside one of the exposed lengths.

"See how the joists run crosswise with the floorboards? They makes perfect little tunnels for rats." Herbert Wenzel held out the candle and motioned for Rudi to kneel beside him and look into the space beneath the floor.

Rudi ventured a careful peek, more than half expecting a rat to jump out at him from the darkness. But all he saw was a series of parallel channels, created by the thick foundation beams that lay side by side beneath the floor, about half an arm's length apart, from one side of the room to the other.

"So now we works together," said the rat catcher, "you, me, and my little dears taking turns—and we sends the ferret in at one end of the tunnel, and the rats bolt out the other, and we catches 'em with these." Herbert Wenzel held up a large net and an empty wire cage. "Which end of the tunnel do you want?"

Rudi felt the blood drain from his head.

The rat catcher burst out in a great guffaw and clapped Rudi on the back. "That's a joke for the new helpers, young master. I can never resist seeing the look on lads' faces. Yours was right up there with the best." And chuckling to himself, Herbert Wenzel stood and carried the net and cage to the opposite side of the room.

"We'll work our way across, one joist at a time. Now, you just bring out my Annalesa nice and gentle, and set her into the first tunnel. She'll know what to do."

Rudi did as he was told.

Annalesa had a long body and short legs, and her pale fur was soft as a rabbit's. She looked something like the weasels and stoats that Rudi often spied on the meadow, but she had a gentle disposition, and she chortled as Rudi rubbed her head and lifted her out of the hutch.

Rudi set the ferret into the opening of the floor. Herbert Wenzel waited at the other end, holding the net. Annalesa immediately disappeared into the darkness, and Rudi could hear her muffled progress across the room as she scrambled along between the joists. A few seconds later, she popped out at the other end and into Herbert Wenzel's waiting hand.

"Nothing there," said Herbert Wenzel. "Send her down the next one." And he released the ferret, who bounded back across the rug and toward Rudi. He scooped her up and sent her again into the darkness beneath the floor, this time one joist to the right.

In short order they had worked halfway across the room. Annalesa was clearly enjoying her game of back-and-forth, but she produced no rats. Rudi was secretly disappointed. He was hoping to see (from his safe position on the opposite side of the room) what the docile Annalesa would do when confronted with a surprised rat.

His disappointment did not last long.

Upon the ferret's very next journey under the floor, there came a wild screech, and then an urgent high-pitched call, something between a squeal and a squawk, and a noisy shuffling and bumping beneath the floorboards.

Annalesa had found her prey.

With a queasy feeling, Rudi realized he could precisely follow the noisy progress of the chase beneath the floor as the animals worked their way toward Herbert Wenzel, who was waiting with his net.

"Got it!" the rat catcher announced, holding up the wriggling net. He shook its contents into the cage, nodded with satisfaction, and made a soft clucking noise, upon which Annalesa emerged from under the floor.

"Good girl," he said, and he rubbed her cheek with his finger. "Now our Beatrice will have her turn."

Thus Rudi, Herbert Wenzel, and the ferrets continued their work, and when they had finished, there were six rats in the cage. Rudi was tempted to brag to his parents about what they had accomplished, but he decided some things were best not bragged about, at least not to his mother.

Next, they prepared a number of traps and laid them in various places under the floor. "For the latecomers," said the rat catcher with a wink, and then they replaced the two floorboards but did not nail them down. "We'll check back in the morning," Herbert Wenzel said. "Shall we visit the neighbors?"

And so they moved from house to house, successfully ferreting rats in nearly every cottage they visited, to the nervous approval of the human inhabitants. They set traps under floors, in the dark corners of barns and sheds, and behind woodpiles. This last task was performed at dusk, so that children would not be in danger of wandering near a snapping trap.

That evening, Rudi gobbled his dinner with zest.

"The boy has worked up quite an appetite," said Oma to his father. "You'd think such unsavory work would have the opposite effect."

Rudi's mother coughed. "Must we have such talk at supper? We have company." And she gave their guest a weak smile.

"Oh, it never bothers me," said Herbert Wenzel. "All in a day's work, I always say. Are there more potatoes, if you please?"

Oma passed him the bowl. "I don't know when else we can talk about it. The boy has been gone all day chasing rats. And catching them, too, I'd say, the way that cage of theirs is filling up."

Mama groaned, and Rudi grinned. Oma clearly delighted in vexing his mother, and Mama never failed to be vexed. Rudi decided that now would not be a good time to tell Mama about the traps lurking beneath the floor, set and ready to spring.

"It goes well, then?" asked Papa, who had no use for delicate conversation. "Rudi, will you forsake the farm to take up the rat catcher's trade?"

Rudi's smile faded as he considered the question. Rat catching (despite its more repulsive aspects) had so far been exceedingly more exciting than hoeing or milking. Such appeal was bound to wear off sooner or later, but there were other advantages. The villagers already looked at him with newfound respect. He was no longer just Rudi Bauer the farmer's son; now he was Rudi the rat catcher's assistant, who was helping to liberate Brixen from its peculiar scourge. And he liked Master Wenzel, so he hesitated to say anything that might sound ungrateful. Still, Rudi knew he could never forsake the farm. It was too much a part of him, and he was too much a part of it.

"No," Rudi finally said. "I mean to say, I like the ferrets, and the work is very . . . interesting . . . but it's more tiring even than plowing. I could never do it regular."

"Thank the saints for that," breathed his mother.

Papa mopped his plate with a bit of bread. "Nothing personal, you understand, Master Wenzel. Our family has tilled this soil, such as it is, for seven generations."

"Oh, I never takes it personal," said the rat catcher. "Very few is cut out for the profession, I'm well aware. The young master here is an able helper, I'll give him that, and my dears have grown right fond of him already. But I can tell he's not a rat catcher at heart, and there's no shame in that. Mayhaps I could have another drop of tea?"

CHAPTER 10

FIRST THING next morning, Rudi again accompanied the rat catcher from house to house, and from woodpile to woodpile, collecting the results of the night's activity.

Herbert Wenzel pulled out a kerchief and wiped his brow. "I'd call that a good night's trapping, lad. Here it is still morning, and it's time to empty our cage."

They hoisted the cage onto a cart and wheeled it to the mayor's house for a tally. Along the way, they were followed by a lively and opinionated audience.

"Look at the number of creatures they've collected," said Mistress Tanner with a note of awe in her voice. "I daresay Master Wenzel knows what he's doing."

Marco the blacksmith grunted. "I notice his cage seems especially full since he's been to your house."

A troop of boys jostled and punched each other in order to get a better look at the cage—which, true enough, was stuffed full with rats of all sizes, colors, and dispositions, squirming and squealing and snapping.

"How many have you caught, Rudi?" asked his friend Konrad. "How do you count them when they won't keep still?"

"What will you do with them now?" asked Roger, who was Konrad's little brother. "Will you kill them? You best should kill them, so they don't come back. How will you kill them?"

Nicolas, the boy who chased imaginary lynxes, pushed out his chest. "Do you need any help? I'm not afeared of them rats."

At which time there came a great racket of squalling and scrabbling from inside the cage, as the knot of rats announced its discomfort and displeasure.

The clutch of boys jumped back with a gasp, and Nicolas turned pale. Herbert Wenzel nudged Rudi and addressed Nicolas. "As a matter of fact, we'll have a task for you in a few minutes' time, if you care to stay for the tally."

Rudi knew very well that Nicolas cared to stay

for the tally. It seemed as if all of Brixen had come out for the tally.

Now Herbert Wenzel addressed the mayor, who stood waiting in his doorway. "Your honor, you'll notice that this here cage is stuffed right full with rats."

The mayor performed an uneasy inspection, and readily agreed.

The rat catcher continued. "In that case, if you don't mind, I propose that we count 'em up this one time, and then mayhaps we can agree that anytime the cage is stuffed right full with rats, the tally will be the same. It would make things easier hereafter."

The mayor regarded the quivering cage. "I think that would be very much appreciated. Wouldn't you say, Master Smith?"

Marco the blacksmith frowned. "It seems to me the rat catcher is trying to save himself some work."

Herbert Wenzel laughed. "True enough, Master Smith. But I'll be saving you some work as well, because the job of tallying these rats will take at least three men. I'll show you what I mean. Hold this." And he pushed a large burlap sack at Marco.

Marco scowled. "They'll chew through this in no time."

"Ah, but they won't," said Herbert Wenzel. "They'll be a good deal confused by the process, and they'll cling to each other and won't nibble a thing, at least not before they're at the bottom of the river." Then he turned to Rudi. "Help him hold it open, lad, if you'd be so kind."

Rudi, assistant rat catcher of Brixen, stepped forward and grasped the sack.

"Now, your honor, you stands right here and counts," said Herbert Wenzel, positioning the mayor between the cage and the open sack. "I'll do the conveying."

Herbert Wenzel pulled on a pair of long cowhide gloves, opened the cage, and commenced with grabbing rats by the squirmy handful and dropping them into the open sack. The mayor counted out loud, assisted by the gaggle of boys, who demonstrated to the whole village their prowess with arithmetic.

"Four! Plus three, that's seven! Ten! Twelve—wait, there's a little one between his fingers—thirteen!"

Thus the noisy tally continued until the cage was nearly empty, and three sacks bulged and squirmed as if they were living creatures themselves.

The rat catcher reached in and chased the last rat around the cage, to the boisterous encouragement of all the boys (and their fathers and uncles as well). When Herbert Wenzel finally grabbed the rat in his gloved hand, a cheer rose from the crowd, and as one they yelled the final tally:

"Sixty-three!"

The mayor joined in the applause. "Well done, Master Wenzel. And from now on we'll assume sixty-three rats in a full cage. Doesn't that sound fair, Master Smith?"

Marco the blacksmith wiped his sweaty brow with a sleeve. "Anything to save us from wrestling with a sack full of sharp-toothed vermin again."

The rat catcher nodded with satisfaction. "Let's say sixty. Makes the accounting easier. And you can keep a running tally of the numbers until I'm finished, if you like. Pay me in a lump sum when the entire job is done."

The mayor removed a small account book from his waistcoat pocket, licked the tip of his pencil, and jotted a note.

There was much applause as Rudi and Herbert Wenzel settled the three sacks onto the cart and proceeded to the footbridge over the deep and swiftly flowing river.

"Where are my helpers?" called Herbert Wenzel. He looked around and caught sight of the group of boys. "I'll be needing some good heavy stones to weigh down these here sacks."

When they were properly weighted and secured, Herbert Wenzel disposed of each quivering sack with a splash. This task was witnessed and verified by the mayor, by Marco the blacksmith, and by the more curious citizens of Brixen, of whom there were quite a few.

The rat catchers kept at their job for four days more, until the entire village had been explored, inspected, and well cleared of rats. They filled and emptied the cage every day, and finally, Herbert Wenzel declared that the task was finished.

During a ragged ceremony in the village square, the mayor thanked Herbert Wenzel and Rudi for their services. He declared that they were owed enough pretty pennies to add up to a goodly number of pretty florins, and he hastened to point out that they had earned every last one. Even Marco the blacksmith remarked on the transformation in the village, and did not begrudge a single penny of his portion.

Rudi felt a tug at his shirt. He looked down to see Susanna Louisa gazing up at him with moony eyes.

"Thank you, Rudi," she whispered. "Thank you for taking away those horrible mouses." And she gave him a wilted bluebell on a broken stem, and ran off to hide behind her mother.

Herbert Wenzel shook Rudi's hand. "Well done,

lad. If you're as able a farmer as you are a rat catcher, I daresay you can be right proud."

His work now finished, Herbert Wenzel settled Annalesa and Beatrice onto his cart and started home to Klausen.

"So," said Oma to Rudi as they watched the rat catcher disappear around a bend in the road. "What do you think, after all that?"

With much relief, and with a handful of coins jingling in his pocket, Rudi said, "I think that sometimes a rat is just a rat."

CHAPTER 11

THE RATS HAD been gone a week, and the village was truly transformed.

Rudi could hear it in the voices of his neighbors, which were full of good humor after weeks of irritable words. He could see it in the way they walked, as if they had become suddenly unburdened.

And Rudi felt it himself. Though it was the height of summer, Rudi felt the energy of springtime in the air. He felt a happy anticipation, as when he heard the river awakening as a trickle beneath the snow, promising to become a torrent. The world was again as it should be, and all was possibility.

Rudi knew there was only one reason for such a feeling of relief and release: The blight of rats had been that awful.

By now, any fear of enchantment or curse had faded from Rudi's mind. He had seen for himself that the scourge was entirely earthly in nature, when he and Herbert Wenzel had dispatched it by entirely earthly means.

Rudi was in such a good mood that he allowed his friends to pull him away from his milking duties. They were as giddy as he was, escaping their own fathers' shops and workbenches to kick a ball or to flirt with the girls who giggled on their way to the well.

"What's the game?" Rudi asked the cluster of boys who were gathered in the village square.

"We're deciding," said Roger, who was six years old and clearly enjoying the chance to mingle with the older boys for once.

"Let's play rat catcher and the rats," announced Nicolas, who had observed enough of the process that now he considered himself an expert. "I'll be the rat catcher."

To which all his friends protested vigorously.

"Why should you be rat catcher?" demanded Konrad. "Just 'cause you're biggest?"

"We could play marbles," suggested Rudi, who'd had enough of rats.

"I should be rat catcher 'cause I thought of it," said Nicolas, ignoring Rudi. "And . . . 'cause I'm biggest."

"So what?" said Roger, stepping forward. "Rudi should be the rat catcher. He's done it for real. He knows how."

Nicolas, confronted with logic, turned red in the face. "Well, if that's so, then you should be the ferret, 'cause you're the smallest. Or maybe you should be the rat in the sack, and we'll throw you into the river."

Rudi tried again. "We could play King of the Mountain."

Roger narrowed his eyes at Nicolas. "Do rats do this?" And he stomped on the bigger boy's foot.

The entire collection of boys erupted into a blurred tussle, punching (mostly air) and kicking (usually themselves) and rolling in the dust. For a fleeting second they reminded Rudi of the rats in their cage.

"So you've decided on your game, then?" he asked, but no one heard. He sighed and wandered off.

Around the corner, Rudi came upon half a dozen girls skipping rope.

"Rudi!" called Susanna Louisa, who was turning one end of the rope. She dropped it and ran toward him. "Come jump with us!"

"Me? I don't know how," he said, but he burst into a wide grin as she took his arm and pulled him toward the group.

The other girls surrounded him, a blur of freckled noses and bouncing braids. Rudi had not much reason to pay attention to girls, but in Brixen every child was known to all, and so he knew these girls, at least by name and family. There was the miller's daughter, Marta, who was very pretty (Rudi had to admit); Clara and Petra, who belonged to Not-So-Old Mistress Gerta; Johanna, the baker's girl, who Konrad was sweet on; and Gretel, who took after her mother (which was lucky, since her father was Marco the blacksmith). They were silly creatures, Rudi thought, but sweet enough, and he was glad to see them acting as carefree as their brothers.

"It's easy," said Susanna Louisa. "Watch." She picked up the loose end of the rope, Clara held the other end, and together they swept it around in wide circles. It beat out a rhythm as it hit the cobbles with each turn.

Now Marta stepped forward and beamed at Rudi, which caused his face to burn. She rocked back and forth on the balls of her feet. Once she found the rhythm of the turning rope, she hopped into its arc and kept the rhythm going with her feet. The other girls chanted as she skipped:

Little children, don't you cry.
Harken to my lullaby.
If you cry, you will despair.
For you'll be sent to the witch's chair.
And if you still have not a care,
You'll be sent to the secret lair.
BOO!

Upon shouting "BOO!" Marta hopped out of the turning rope, laughing. She tugged at Rudi's sleeve. "Your turn!"

Should he? Rudi wasn't eager to embarrass himself by failing at something a slip of a girl could do without a second thought.

Marta fluttered her eyelids at him. He decided it would be worth a try. Besides, how hard could it be? With a quick glance around to satisfy himself that none of the boys were watching, Rudi began to nod his head and tap his foot in time with the turning rope.

The girls applauded to encourage him, and soon they were clapping in unison.

They began to chant. "Rudi, Ru-di, Ru-di!"

He jumped.

But his timing was off, and immediately the rope became tangled at his feet. The girls dissolved into fits of giggles, but then they started clapping again, and the rope was turned once more.

"Ru-di, Ru-di, Ru-di!"

He inhaled deeply, and this time he watched the rope carefully, and timed his leap perfectly. He skipped the rope while the girls clapped out the rhythm and chanted his name, and then they sang out once more:

> The secret lair is cold and damp.
> Has not a blanket nor a lamp.
> Sing these words and count to three,
> Sing these words and you'll be free:
> 'Home is where I want to be.
> At my hearth with a cup of tea.'
> One . . . two . . . THREE!

Just as the girls yelled "THREE!" Rudi laughed, and he lost his rhythm. The rope slapped his ankles and stopped.

The girls erupted into applause once more, and behind them Rudi made out one or two mothers standing in their doorways, doing the same. His face burned, but then he gave them all a sweeping bow. He was having too much fun, and he decided he didn't care who saw him.

"Who's next?" he called. He took Clara's end of the rope and dutifully turned it until every girl had had her turn. Then they all tumbled around the corner and into the square, where they dipped their cupped hands into the fountain for a cool drink.

"Rudi?" said Susanna Louisa, wiping her chin with her sleeve. "Is the witch's chair real? You know—the one in the song?"

Rudi considered her question. The song was an old one, and he had known it by heart since he was very small. Just like the legends of the Brixen Witch and her treasure, he had always assumed it was nothing more than a story. But now . . .

"I'm not sure," he said, because he remembered being eight years old, and knew that when an eight-year-old asks a question, she wants to be told the truth. "It could be real, I suppose. I've never seen it, though."

This seemed to satisfy Susanna Louisa, who ran off to join her friends. But Rudi was not satisfied. He decided he would ask Oma, because something told him she would know the answer, and she would tell him the truth. That was one trait old people and children held in common, Rudi observed: Neither was afraid of the truth. He wondered why people changed in the middle years of life, and why they changed back again later. Then he wondered why people bothered changing at all, if they just came back to the way they'd been in the first place.

His musings were interrupted by a shrill noise.

Rudi blinked and looked about. The little girls were scattering and screaming. The noise pierced Rudi's ears, and he could not make out any real words. He reached for a blur of a pinafore and grabbed hold of an arm. The arm belonged to Marta.

"What's wrong?" he asked her.

Marta looked at him, her lovely eyes filled with fear. Her mouth opened, but no sound came out. So she pointed, and Rudi's gaze followed her outstretched finger.

And then he saw them. Spilling down the drainpipes of the village hall. Skittering over the stone walls of the churchyard. Swimming through the fountain, fouling its pure water.

"It can't be," Rudi exclaimed.

But no one heard him. And finally the screams gathered themselves into one terrible, ruinous word.

"Rats!"

CHAPTER 12

THAT NIGHT, a summer storm raged.

The wind screamed down the mountain and into the village. It blasted its way down chimneys, blowing ashes onto hearths, so that dogs awoke with a yelp and their masters jumped out of their chairs to stomp on the glowing embers before their rugs caught fire.

The thunder shook grandfathers out of their beds and caused babies to wail in their cradles. Slashes of lightning split the night, illuminating every stone and every blade of grass.

Yet those who dared peek through their shutters beheld a black and cloudless sky.

Some villagers thought they saw shadows crossing the moon, and were convinced they saw not passing storm clouds but the witch taking flight. Others swore that the flashes of light seen upon the Berg were not wildfires ignited by the lightning but the witch's bonfires. Tonight, they whispered, she was celebrating her dominion over all of Brixen.

Even the rats seemed fearful of the witch, or whatever force of nature worked its wicked magic upon the land. They had been unnaturally bold upon their reappearance, hardly bothering to hide or skulk. But now, while the storm prevailed, there was not a rat to be seen.

In the Bauer cottage, Oma rocked so hard that her chair inched its way across the room.

Mama and Papa fretted and paced as the wind carried upon it the clang of cowbells and a chorus of restless lowing. Finally unable to contain their worry, they threw on their cloaks, lit a lantern, and ventured into the darkness and toward the barn.

"They'll be all right," said Rudi as he peered out the window. "Won't they?"

Oma snorted. "They'll be fine, the poor dumb creatures."

"I don't mean the cows," Rudi said.

"Neither do I," she snapped. Then she sighed. "They're only going twenty steps, child. I should think they won't be hit by lightning in twenty steps."

Rudi didn't say it out loud, but he wasn't only worried about the lightning.

"It's just as well they're gone," said Oma, and she stopped rocking and fixed her gaze upon Rudi. "What do you suppose is happening here? No stories, now, or vague excuses. Tell me."

Rudi had been afraid to even think about the new plague of rats, or the storm, or what they might mean, much less to say a word out loud to anyone. But now he felt an odd sort of relief at Oma's request, and the words spilled from his mouth.

"I don't know what's happening. I wish I did! The rats are *not* just rats. . . . There must be a curse after all. Is it my fault? Because of the coin? But I've heard no strange singing. I've had no nightmares for months. Doesn't that mean the witch got her coin back? I thought that meant she got her coin back."

"You're babbling," said Oma. "But it's a truthful babble, I know. You never could spin a lie. Tell me, then: If the witch has her coin, why is the village being tormented so?"

Lightning crackled and flashed outside, as if to underscore her question.

Rudi bit his lip. "I thought perhaps you would know why."

"Me?" sniffed Oma. "How would I know? I've never seen such a curse as rats. And for what? What have we done now to rile the witch so badly?"

Then an idea came to Rudi, as easily as if it had been there all along. "Do you suppose someone else has found the coin after all this time, and has brought it back to Brixen?" Why hadn't he thought of that before? It made perfect sense. And it gave him a glimmer of hope. Perhaps this was not his fault after all.

But Oma shook her head. "I would have heard about it. No one in Brixen could keep such a secret for long. Besides, why would the witch torment the entire village for the foolish mistake of one person? Why not simple, straightforward nightmares, such as you had? Perhaps the witch has not recovered her coin after all. Since the nightmares didn't have the desired result, perhaps she is trying something new."

Rudi gulped. "This is all my fault, then?"

"It seems so," said Oma, but her voice was kind.

The glimmer of hope sputtered and died in the pit of Rudi's stomach.

"And yet . . . it doesn't fit," continued Oma, rocking harder, as if it helped her to think. "Rats. That doesn't sound like our witch." She drummed her fingers on the arms of her chair, muttering to herself, but her words were lost in a rumble of thunder.

Finally, she looked up at Rudi, and her eyes shone. "Do you remember what Herbert Wenzel said?" She pointed a finger at Rudi. "He said that rats were not the witch's sort of hex."

Rudi thought for a moment, and then he nodded. "Yes. I remember."

Oma nodded too, which started her chair to rocking again. "The rat catcher is right. Our witch is not so crude as that." She scowled again in thought. "And yet . . . only the witch has enough power to bring on such a curse."

Rudi frowned in puzzlement. "Only the witch has enough power for such a curse . . . and yet it's not her curse? What does it mean? Who else could be at work?" And then the answer came to him. "Her servant?"

Oma shuddered and shook her head. "Impossible. The only power he possesses is that which *she* grants him, and believe me: the Brixen Witch would never grant so much power to her servant."

Rudi was beginning to understand why so many people learned to avoid the truth. The truth could be maddening and unpleasant. Still, he would not turn away from it. "What do we do now?" he asked.

Oma sighed. "There's nothing to do but wait. Whatever is at work here, it likes giving signs. Rats. Thunder and lightning. Something tells me there will be another sign before too long."

They sat in silence for a moment as the wind howled over their heads.

Then Oma stood, hobbled across the room, and opened the door to the fury of the storm. "There's something more than the witch at work here." She slammed the door against the night and turned to face Rudi. "You think the witch is trouble? She's nothing compared with a menace we don't know."

CHAPTER 13

"WE'VE BEEN robbed!" growled Marco the blacksmith. "I'll go to Klausen myself if I must, and I'll drag that swindler back to Brixen and shake every last penny from his pockets."

"You'll do no such thing," said Otto the baker. "Herbert Wenzel performed the task we paid him to perform. You watched him with your own eyes."

An emergency meeting had been assembled. Rudi guessed that half the populace of Brixen had packed itself into the village hall, while the other half (Mama and Papa among them) remained home to swat at rats. Now that the storm had passed, the vile creatures had returned to their nasty work, chewing whatever cheese, ham hock, or mattress they could find. And they seemed to be finding them all.

"Then where have these rats come from?" said Marco. "Can't get rid of every last rat, he said. I say he left some behind on purpose, so we would call him back and pay him twice. I warned you this would happen."

Arguments and discussions rippled through the crowd like wind through the trees.

"Nonsense," said Otto. "Even if he left a few pairs of rats behind, how could they have overrun the town again in a matter of days? Not even rats are *that* busy."

"So you're an expert on rats now, are you?" said Marco, growing red in the face.

Mistress Tanner shook her finger at the blacksmith. "Have you forgotten last night already? That storm was the witch's doing, and if you ask me, so are the rats. But all you can think of is money. I'd like to see you try and venture to Klausen while the witch is abroad."

"Why shouldn't I?" answered Marco. "I've done nothing to vex the witch. Has anyone here done so?"

There was a wave of muttering and emphatic head shaking. Only Rudi knew the answer to Marco's question, but he could not find the courage to speak up.

The blacksmith continued. "Of course we haven't. And yet she torments us. Rats. Storms. Why?"

Marco stopped in midbreath. His eyebrows bunched together. Rudi thought he could almost hear the rusty gears creaking inside the man's head.

And then the gears clanked into place, and Marco's face became a picture of triumph. "Of course! There can be only one reason for this new plague of rats. Herbert Wenzel is in league with the witch!"

The muttering erupted into gasps and exclamations. The mayor banged his gavel, but no one paid attention.

"Now see here!" said Otto the baker. "I've known Herbert Wenzel nearly my entire life. He's no more in league with the witch than your own children are, you scruffy oaf of a blacksmith!"

Rudi felt a wave of unease rising in his chest.

"Oma!" He shook her shoulder. "Say something."

"Me? These fools aren't listening to each other. Why would they listen to me?"

Rudi winced in frustration. What about Herbert Wenzel? It was not right that an innocent man should have his name dishonored simply because a collection of panicked villagers had been tormented to their wits' end. Someone had to speak up.

Before he could lose his nerve, Rudi pushed his way to the platform at the front of the hall, snatched the gavel from the mayor's hand, and smacked it on the table with such force that its handle broke with a *CRACK*.

The room fell silent. Mouths hung open, and all eyes were upon Rudi.

He cleared his throat, and then he forced himself to speak.

"Master Wenzel is not in league with the witch. I worked alongside him for six days, in the worst conditions. Yet he was nothing but patient and good humored. He is an honest and decent man, and I cannot let you talk of him this way."

Rudi looked down at the room full of stunned faces and decided that, while he had their attention, he should make good use of it.

"Nor are these rats the witch's doing," he continued, with a glance toward Oma, who nodded her encouragement. "Master Wenzel told me so, and of all people, he knows about rats. I believe him, and so should you."

Otto the baker applauded. "The boy speaks sense."

"The boy is only a boy," declared Marco. "What does he know of the witch and her cohorts? And you, Master Otto—perhaps you've known the rat catcher all your life, but he lives afar, and you can only vouch for his behavior a few days out of every year. How can you know what he does in Klausen when you're not there?"

There was a new assortment of murmurs and head scratching. Rudi caught sight of Not-So-Old-Mistress Gerta whispering into Oma's ear. Then the two women pushed through the crowd and out the nearest door.

"I sorely hate to say it, but I think the blacksmith here is right." It was Mistress Tanner again. "All my respect to young Rudi here, who's an able lad and is kind to my Susanna Louisa, as silly a child as children come. But bless me! How can Herbert Wenzel claim the rats are not the witch's doing? They can be nothing else!"

"He seemed like such an honest fellow," said the mayor, scratching his bald head.

Mistress Tanner snorted. "How else would you expect a servant of the witch to act? Such folk are cunning and sly. Of course they'll act honest and decent, so's to lull you into complacency. Then they lay a hex on you that sticks forever."

The crowd gasped as one. Now that Oma was gone, Rudi was beginning to feel quite lonely and small.

"Well spoken, my dear Mistress Tanner!" declared Marco. "Besides, young Master Rudi here is not exactly an innocent bystander. Did he not also profit from the rat catcher's escapade? Here he is, with quite a full purse to show for his activities. I'll wager he stands to earn even more if the rat catcher comes back a second time."

This was too much for Rudi. He dug in his pocket for the few pennies he carried and tossed them onto the table.

"Here! I earned three florins working for Master Wenzel. The rest is at home, but you can have that too." Rudi forced back the angry tears that welled up behind his eyes. He drew himself up and spoke in a voice that was as loud and as steady as he could manage.

"Master Wenzel is not in league with the witch. He had nothing to do with the blight of rats, either before or now. I swear this as true fact." Rudi could hardly believe such bold words were coming from his own mouth, but he dared not stop himself. He must admit to everyone, in a clear voice and in a public place, that the blight of rats was no one's fault but his own.

"See what I mean?" said Marco. "The lad is twelve years old. How can he swear such a thing? He's only making noise."

"No!" Rudi protested. "I'll tell you how I know."

"Leave the boy alone," declared Otto the baker. He scraped the coins off the table and handed them back to Rudi. "He earned his wage honestly. Besides, it's no use to argue over the cause of this blight. The question is, how do we get rid of it?"

From somewhere in the room came a persistent thumping. Rudi looked around, as did everyone in the hall. Then Rudi saw that the thumping was caused by a walking stick, as a hand methodically tapped it on the floorboards.

Little by little, the crowd fell silent.

"If I may," said the stranger who held the stick, "I can get rid of your rats once and for all."

CHAPTER 14

THE CROWD stared openmouthed at the man who had spoken.

From his position on the mayor's platform, Rudi had a clear view of the stranger, who wore a drab oilskin cloak and a tattered hat that partly hid his face. Something about him was unsettlingly familiar, but Rudi could not recall how or why.

Finally, the mayor cleared his throat and performed his official duty. "Welcome, sir, to Brixen. What brings you to our village, and how is it you know our particular . . . situation and how to solve it?"

The stranger gave a nod. "You honor me with your kind greeting, Master Mayor. I am but a traveler, on my way to Petz. Have you been to Petz? As I walked through your lovely village, I could not help but notice two things. Firstly, there was no one about, which I thought quite odd on such a fine day as this."

Rudi glanced up. Rain was beginning to batter the windows.

The unsettled feeling churned in Rudi's stomach. Where had he seen this man before? The memory he wanted remained stubbornly beyond his grasp.

"Secondly," said the stranger, "there seemed to be quite a few, er, vermin about, and of a very bold nature, if I may say. In fact, in all my travels I've never seen such a display. Do you know I just watched a rat scamper along a clothesline as if it were solid ground?" He pointed vaguely toward the outdoors as if to prove his claim.

Was that a bit of color Rudi glimpsed beneath the man's cloak?

The stranger continued. "Then I heard a hubbub coming from this hall, so I thought I'd step inside to see what sort of festivity might be under way, and—well, I walked into the midst of your conversation, and I hope you'll excuse me for that. But if I may say, what a lucky day for you as well as for me! As it happens, I have quite a way with pests of all kinds."

"We've heard that before," grumbled Marco. "You don't know a scoundrel from Klausen named Wenzel, do you?"

"I'm afraid not," said the stranger. "At any rate, here I am. At your service." He took off his threadbare hat and bowed as best he could in the crush of villagers.

Rudi gasped.

It was the face in the window. The man in Rudi's nightmares, with hair like a thistle burr and a shirt of motley patches hiding beneath his cloak.

This was the witch's servant.

"Oma?" Rudi croaked, but she had gone off with Not-So-Old-Mistress Gerta and had not returned.

Why had he come? What did he want? Would he finally bring his wrath down upon Rudi for taking the witch's coin? And yet, though Rudi stood in full view on the platform, the stranger showed no sign of knowing him.

But Rudi had earned the stranger's wrath, while his neighbors had not. He opened his mouth to expose the malevolence in their midst, but he could not force out a sound.

What would be the use anyway? Marco the smith had already bullied nearly the entire hall into believing that Rudi was nothing but a silly child who craved attention. They wouldn't believe a word Rudi said, least of all a claim that the witch's true servant was standing among them now.

"And how do you propose to rid us of this

pestilence?" said the mayor, and Rudi feared that the villagers were so desperate for relief from the rats that they were likely to agree to almost anything.

"I have devised a practice all my own," said the stranger. "I can explain it if you wish, but does it matter how? The proof will be in the result. Let me add: I can give you an absolute guarantee."

At these words, even Marco the blacksmith appeared interested. "Every last rat?"

The stranger nodded. "Every last rat, once and for all."

Dread gripped Rudi's throat so that he could scarcely breathe. Such a promise could never be fulfilled. Not by earthly means.

Then Marco's eyes narrowed. "One moment, sir. A guarantee is all well and good, but at what cost? We've already paid a pretty penny—for empty promises." He cast a dark eye at Rudi, who glared defiantly back.

"Ah yes, well," said the stranger, nodding politely toward the blacksmith. "Understandable, I'm sure. And yet, from the looks of things hereabouts, may I say you seem to be running short on choices?"

The mayor cleared his throat and pulled at his mustache. "We will hear you out, sir, but you must know that Brixen is not a wealthy town.

Our coffers, quite frankly, lie even closer to empty than usual, due to . . . recent expenses. So then, if you'd be so kind. Before we continue this discussion, perhaps we should discuss a price for your services."

A grin spread across the stranger's face, and his eyes gleamed. "A price? Well, yes. There's always a price."

"Let's hear it then, man," declared Marco. "How much do you plan to swindle us for?"

"Master Smith, mind your tongue," interrupted Mistress Tanner. "Our visitor has been nothing but good natured and agreeable. And he is offering to solve our desperate problem. Goodness knows we haven't been able to solve it any other way." And she turned toward the stranger and curtsied. "Excuse that dunderhead, kind sir. There's one in every village, and he's ours."

Rudi could scarcely believe his ears. Wasn't it Mistress Tanner who'd admonished him only a few moments ago that any servant of the witch would be sly and cunning? Would lull a person into complacency?

The stranger waved his hand. "Never trouble yourself, mistress. The gentlemen are right to ask the question. Yet no one would expect the good blacksmith to forge a set of hinges and hasps without proper compensation for his trouble and his skill. The more delicate the task, the higher the payment, is that not so? It's no different for myself. Surely anyone can understand that."

The crowd gave a collective shrug, and then there came a scattering of nods.

"Spoken well and plainly," said the mayor from the platform. "Which we all applaud, and if you truly can perform this service—and offer an absolute guarantee—the entire village of Brixen would be most grateful, I'm sure. Still—what *is* your fee?"

The stranger smiled kindly. "Your situation appears to be most dire."

"Yes," said the mayor. "It is. Please, name your price."

Now the stranger's eyes shone in muted triumph. "My price," he said, "is one golden guilder."

A huge commotion erupted in the hall. Villagers gasped in shock, and some recoiled from the stranger in their midst.

With sudden and horrifying clarity, Rudi understood everything. The witch had not recovered her coin after all. Crude hex or no, she had indeed sent the rats, and now her servant, to root out the coin and return it to her at last.

"You must be mad!" exclaimed Marco.

"I'm sure we heard him wrong," said Mistress Tanner. "No one has seen an actual golden guilder in generations, much less used one as currency. They're too precious and rare. Guilder coins are made of mostly copper nowadays."

"He knows that," barked Marco. "Even where he comes from." Then he turned toward the stranger. "Where *do* you come from?"

Mistress Tanner gave the stranger a nervous little curtsy. "Isn't that what you meant, kind sir? A copper guilder?"

The stranger's smile did not fade. "No, mistress. You heard me well."

Mistress Tanner turned pale, and another commotion erupted in the hall.

"You must come from the moon, then," said Marco, his face growing red. "In these parts, one golden guilder is worth upwards of ten thousand florins."

"May as well ask for the crown jewels," declared Otto the baker. "Because we haven't got them, neither."

The mayor banged the head of his broken gavel until he could be heard. "Such an amount is quite impossible, sir! Even if we piled every coin, every scrap of gold, every ring from every finger, it would not add up to one golden guilder."

"Nevertheless," said the stranger, "that is my price." He settled his hat upon his head. "You may contemplate my offer. I'll be back tomorrow." The stranger tucked his walking stick under his arm and strode toward the door.

"Wait!" called Rudi from the platform. "We'll pay your price. We'll pay you one golden guilder."

CHAPTER 15

THE STRANGER turned. He cocked an eyebrow at Rudi, but still his face betrayed no recognition. Then he bowed. "Smart lad. I like you."

"But you must give us three days."

The stranger considered for a moment. "Very well," he said finally. "You can pay me after three days." And he left the hall.

The villagers stood in stunned silence for a heartbeat. Then they erupted into shouts of anger and distress.

"You fool of a boy!" said Marco. "What were you thinking?"

"I'd say he's a clever boy," said Otto the baker. "He's given the stranger three days to understand how preposterous his request is. Now when he comes back we can have a real discussion."

Rudi shook his head. "That's not what I meant. I know where —"

"What's there to discuss?" said Mistress Tanner. "How many different ways we can't pay that man?"

Marco scowled. "A golden guilder! What does that rogue take us for? We could pay Herbert Wenzel to catch rats every day until the freeze comes, and it would not cost a fraction of that amount."

Rudi tried again. "But I can get —"

"There's something disquieting about that man," said Mistress Tanner with a shudder. "Did you notice how cold the room became when he was here?"

"That's because he is the witch's true servant."

No one moved. No one breathed. Rudi himself could scarcely believe the words he'd just uttered.

Marco pushed forward. "How do you know this?"

Rudi wished Mama and Papa were there. He wished Oma would come back. But he was on his own. "I've seen him before. He wore the same shirt of motley patches."

The crowd grew restless. "I saw only a drab cloak," muttered one man, but Rudi saw fear in his eyes.

"And the room grew cold. Did you not say so just now?" said Rudi.

"It might have been only a draft," said Mistress Tanner, but she could not meet Rudi's gaze.

"The boy speaks truth," said Otto the baker, stepping onto the platform and placing a hand on Rudi's shoulder. "We all know the old stories. I've heard the witch's servant described just that way, by my own grandmother when I was a boy. He's menaced us before, and he's doing it again."

"But why would the witch send her servant to Brixen now?" said another voice. "Haven't we been cursed enough?"

Only Rudi could answer such questions. And so, with a mixture of trepidation and relief, he finally confessed his sin.

"There truly is a golden guilder. An enchanted coin. The witch's coin." He told them everything, leaving out no detail—how he stumbled upon the coin that day in October, when he was on the mountain. How he tried to return it the very next morning but lost it in the avalanche. And how, as a result, he had brought this torment upon his good and decent neighbors.

Rudi held his breath and waited for the response he knew must come.

"You?" said Mistress Tanner in disbelief. "*You* are the cause of all our grief?"

Rudi gulped and nodded. "But I can—"

"Just a moment!" thundered Marco, and he

pointed an accusing finger at Rudi. "You stole the witch's gold?"

"No!" said Rudi. "I mean yes — I mean it was an accident!"

"Leave the boy alone," said Otto. "He just told you what happened. It was an innocent blunder. Besides, what's done is done."

Rudi tried again. "I know where to look —"

"Well, isn't that a fine surprise," said Marco, and a grin spread across his face. "Our boy here stole the witch's gold."

"He's telling stories," someone said. "Don't your cows need milking, lad? Go home to your chores now, and let adults tend to adult matters."

Rudi opened his mouth to protest, when there came a gust of damp air as the rear door opened.

It was Oma. She looked from face to face, frowning in puzzlement. Then she made her way to the front of the hall as the villagers stepped aside to let her pass. When she reached the platform step, she motioned for Rudi to help her up.

"Where were you?" he whispered to her. "You won't believe what's been happening."

"Wouldn't I?" she said. "Master Mayor, a word, if you please."

The mayor bustled over. He and Oma conferred for a moment in hushed tones. Then the mayor's eyes grew wide, and his face grew pale.

Oma stepped to the front of the platform, raised a hand, and waited. Little by little the crowd noticed, and it hushed itself into silence.

"I have sorry news," she announced. "Old Mistress Gerta has died."

The crowd gasped.

"It comes as no real surprise," Oma said. "She was the oldest in the village, and she'd been ill since the spring, as we all know. It was simply her time."

There came another gust of wind as the door opened once more. "The rats! I've come to warn you all. It was the rats!"

Not-So-Old Mistress Gerta stood in the open doorway. "My dear old mother, falling victim to this nasty, evil pestilence! They tortured her day and night with their scurrying and their skittering and their gnawing and their nibbling. The rats killed my mother!" And she blew her nose and wiped her red eyes. "I must get back home. But I'm telling you all. Don't think you won't be next!"

With a sob, Not-So-Old Mistress Gerta left the hall, and the door slammed shut behind her.

A commotion erupted then.

"I must go home too!" said one voice.

"My babies!" cried another.

"Bring the stranger back," said Mistress Tanner. "We have no choice. Pay him whatever he wants!"

Oma nudged Rudi. "The stranger?"

"The witch's servant. He was here! He promised to rid us of the rats for good. For the price of a golden guilder."

Oma's eyebrows shot up. "A golden guilder? That can mean only one thing."

Rudi gave a fretful nod. "The coin is still missing. It must still be buried on the mountain after all. Who knows what the witch and her servant will do if they don't get what they want? We must find the coin. *I* must find it. I'm the only one who knows where I dropped it."

Oma sighed. "And so you must."

The mayor pounded his broken gavel once more, but no one paid any heed.

"Poor, poor Gerta," wailed Mistress Tanner. "To see her dear old mother done in by rats! I wouldn't wish such a fate on anyone!" Her gaze fell upon Marco the blacksmith. "Not even you!"

Once more, Oma stepped forward and raised a hand, until a restless quiet settled over the crowd.

"Let's not lose our heads," she said. "Mistress Gerta is distressed and full of grief. She cannot say for certain that the rats killed her mother."

"Can you say for certain that they didn't?" said Mistress Tanner, who was close to tears herself. "If that stranger truly is the witch's servant, all the more reason to pay him what he asks and be rid of him as well as the rats. We must search every corner of every house. We must find whatever gold we can, and hope it's enough to satisfy him."

Heads nodded in agreement, and the crowd began to buzz with renewed energy.

"I have an antique gold florin that my grandfather gave me when I was a boy," said an old man. "It's a collector's item! Minted during the reign of King Balthazar the Elder, before he went mad. I'm willing to part with it for a good cause."

Rudi's stomach flipped. They did not understand that the witch and her servant would be satisfied with nothing but the golden guilder itself. He tried once more. "But the stranger only wants—"

"You see?" said another voice. "Master Mayor, we may yet collect a golden guilder's worth. And we have three days to do it."

"Please!" said Rudi, but no one heard.

"Save your breath," Oma said to him. "Let them busy themselves digging for their treasures and their trinkets. In the meantime, you can do what you must do."

The mayor held up his hands to quiet the crowd. "It's decided, then. Find whatever gold and silver you can spare, and hold nothing back. We'll reconvene here in three days' time. Good luck to us all."

And with a bang of the broken gavel, the meeting was adjourned.

CHAPTER 16

THE DOORS of the hall were flung open, and the villagers shuffled out into the misty morning.

Rudi and Oma lagged behind, and made their way home through an eerie quiet. Where had everyone gone so quickly? Perhaps the spitting rain had chased even the children indoors. Perhaps the news of Old Mistress Gerta had already made its rounds, and the village had begun its mourning. Perhaps everyone had decided that they'd finally lost their battle with the rats, and so had finally lost heart. Rudi couldn't blame his neighbors for hiding indoors. He wished he could do the same.

"No," he said to himself. "Now is my chance to make things right." He dared not think about what might happen if he could not find the coin. He would find it. He *must* find it.

They came upon Old Mistress Gerta's house, where the doorway was already draped with black cloth.

"Let me see how Gerta and her children are faring," said Oma. "Go now. Gather what you need to find that coin." Oma glanced up at the Berg, which loomed over Brixen like a storm cloud. "I'm glad it's you going up there. If anyone can find it, you can." She patted his cheek and disappeared into the house.

Rudi continued on his way, wishing he felt as confident as Oma did. He crossed the village square and was nearly home when he heard a curious noise. He looked around, and his brow furrowed. There was something familiar about the sound.

Then, with a sudden dread, Rudi knew. It was the tuneless song he had heard months ago; the music of the enchanted coin; the distant playing of a pennywhistle.

No. Not a pennywhistle this time. What was it?

A fiddle.

Someone was scraping a bow across the strings of a fiddle. The sound echoed off the cobbles and the timbers, so that Rudi could not tell where it was coming from. The curious music grated against his eardrums, but it was also oddly soothing. He went to cover his ears, but then he stopped, unable to resist its plaintive wail.

The music seemed to have the same effect on others. Rudi could see faces in every window as his neighbors strained to hear where the music might be coming from.

The question was answered presently, for around a corner came the fiddler in his drab cloak and threadbare hat. A gust of wind caught the cloak as he walked, revealing his patchy shirt of red and yellow and faded blue. The unearthly melody flowed behind him on the air as he strode through the village square.

"Is that scoundrel still here?" came a voice behind Rudi. It belonged to Marco, who stood with a pickax on his shoulder.

"Apparently so," said another voice. It was Otto, and he carried a shovel. "We thought you might want some company up there," he said to Rudi, and he cocked his head toward the Berg. Beside him, Marco gave a nod.

Relief and gratitude flooded through Rudi, and he nodded back.

At that moment, from every direction, there came a series of muffled shrieks and cries. A moment later, every door on the square flew open, and every window swung outward, and from every house came the rats.

They leapt over the thresholds; they scuttled

down from the thatch. They came spilling out of woodpiles, and they sprang from every shed. They tumbled through the square, from out of every alley and lane. And then they all stopped, as if to listen. Some even rose on their hind legs, twitching their ears and whiskers. Then, as if the hundreds of creatures had suddenly become a single living thing, every rat turned and ran in the same direction. In the direction of the music.

"Toward the footbridge!" someone called, and Rudi saw that it was true. He followed the streaming rats, as did the other villagers. He turned a corner and watched the fiddler stride away to the end of the lane and across the footbridge. The rats followed him as if they were enchanted.

Well, they *are* enchanted, Rudi thought. And then he had another fearful realization. The witch's servant was fulfilling his end of the bargain without waiting for Rudi to produce the coin. The evil stranger was demonstrating his power, not just over the rats but over the whole village. If there had been any question before, there was none now: The witch had indeed granted fearsome power to her servant, and together they held sway over all of Brixen. There could be only one way out, and Rudi had only three days.

"What just happened?" asked Mistress Tanner, who stood in the lane with all the others, blinking the mist out of her eyes. They watched the rats stream after the fiddler, up the path that crossed the meadow, until they disappeared over a rise.

"Eeek!" came a small voice. Susanna Louisa clutched her mother's skirts as one furry straggler scurried past her feet and over the bridge, after the others. Then the town was left silent except for the tumbling stream and the fading music of the fiddle.

And then a great cheer arose. The grown-ups whooped, and the children danced, and they all embraced each other and threw their caps into the air.

Rudi felt a hand on his shoulder. He turned to see his mother blinking tears from her eyes. Or perhaps it was the rain.

"They're gone!" Mama said. "Bless us, I think they're really gone." And she hugged him, and wiped her eyes, and Rudi had not the heart to tell her what a dubious blessing it was.

Papa stood beside her. "I wouldn't believe it if I hadn't seen it myself." Then he turned to Rudi and handed him a shovel and his best hunting knife. "Oma tells me you're going on an . . . excursion. I wish I could join you, but your Mama and the cows need looking after." He reached out, ready to ruffle Rudi's hair, but then he stopped. Instead, he held out his hand. "Good luck, son."

Rudi lifted his chin, and he shook his father's strong hand, but he could meet his gaze for only a moment, lest he embarrass himself with the sniffle that threatened to escape. He busied himself lashing the knife in its sheath to his belt.

The mayor came bustling over, his mustache quivering. "Well, now. Say what you will about that stranger, but he does work quickly."

"And we'd better do likewise," muttered Otto to his companions. "If it's a golden guilder the witch wants, then let's go find it."

Marco stepped up and clapped Rudi on the back. "Anyone with the nerve to steal the witch's gold is all right in my book. Besides, I damned well won't pay that thief a single penny from my own pocket. Lead the way up the mountain, boy."

CHAPTER 17

AND SO RUDI led Marco and Otto up the mountain. As they climbed, the rain sputtered and stopped, and the day grew warm.

The fiddler had led the rats this way. The path was pocked with a thousand tiny paw prints, where it hadn't been swept smooth by a thousand scaly tails.

Rudi shuddered, and was grateful for his companions. Marco had the brawn of three men, if not quite the brains of one. Otto looked nearly as soft as the dough he kneaded, but he was an experienced traveler, and he knew the mountain well. Together they would find the coin. They *must* find the coin.

They lost the fiddler's trail when they entered the shade of the forest, but Rudi had no desire to follow the fiddler. When the time came, Rudi knew, the fiddler would come to him.

Before long, Rudi led Marco and Otto out of the forest and into the clearing, where the path continued up and around the treeline toward the high meadow. As he had done the last time he'd been there, those many months before, Rudi stopped and surveyed the view. In one direction he could see all the way to the valley below and to the village, which lay nestled between green hills. In the other direction, the Berg loomed closer than ever, black and cold, even in the heat of July.

"Here," announced Rudi. "Here is where I climbed up." And he pointed straight up the mountain, across the slope of loose rock, where he'd had his misadventure.

Otto shaded his eyes and craned his neck. "Why didn't you go that way?" He pointed to the right, where the trail was clear and safe, curving back and forth across the slope and up to the high meadow.

Marco burst out in a laugh. "Let me understand this. Hunters and cowherds and travelers have trodden these paths, and worn them bare, day after day, year upon year, for perhaps a thousand years? And then one day *you* come along and decide you know a better way." He shook his head, and his laugh became an exasperated sigh. "I'm beginning to think I was wrong about you, boy."

Rudi's face grew hot. He deserved that. He'd been proud and foolhardy, and ever since, he'd paid for it. He tried to maintain his dignity.

"All right, it was a mistake. But what's done is done. We need to retrace my steps and find where I slipped, so we know where to look for the coin."

"That won't be easy," said Otto, surveying the field of scree. "Last winter's snows would have piled up and shifted the gravel. Any footprints you might have left will be gone by now."

Rudi knew Otto was right. For all the world, it looked as if not a soul had set foot on that field of rock since the day it was set down by the hand of God. He needed something else. A landmark of some sort.

Rudi looked around and tried to get his bearings. He studied every boulder for a clue that might jog his memory. But every rock looked just like every other rock. He inspected the trees at the base of the field of scree, to see if he'd left any gash or scar when he'd crashed to a stop. But he found not a mark. It was as if he'd never been there.

Rudi swallowed a groan of despair. He could not be defeated already. The stakes were too high.

"Well?" said Marco. "Where did you fall, then?"

Rudi could only shrug and scratch his head.

Marco snorted. "This field must be more than an acre in size. How are we supposed to sift through an acre of rock to find a coin the size of a chestnut?"

Otto held up his hands. "Let's be sensible about this. Rudi, what else do you remember about that day?"

Rudi tried to think. "I know I was on this slope, and when I slipped, the trees stopped me. And I dropped the coin just before I hit the trees."

Otto pointed. "So it must be somewhere near the trees." He walked away from Rudi, using long measured strides, and counted his steps. He stopped at the far end of the thin stand of trees. "And the trees span twenty paces. So we start searching here. Twenty paces across and perhaps five paces upslope. Agreed?"

Rudi sighed and nodded in relief. A plan.

Marco nodded as well. "It'll have to do. Each of you start at one end, and I'll take the middle." And he raised his pickax, ready to make the first strike.

"Wait!" said Rudi. "While you search, you must also listen. The coin sings."

Marco and Otto blinked at him.

Rudi shrugged. "It's enchanted. It wants to be found. Its music sounds something like that fiddle music we heard."

"Well, strike me deaf and blind," declared Marco. "What have I signed up for?"

Then he swung his pickax, and Otto and Rudi scraped with their shovels, and the mountain echoed with the clang of metal on rock. If the coin was sleeping there, Rudi thought, this noise would surely awaken it. Or at least, he fervently hoped so.

Hours passed, and hope faded, for Rudi heard no singing, and he saw no glint of metal. The sun dropped lower in the sky, until it slid behind the peak of the Berg and cast the field of loose rock into shadow. Still, the coin was not found. The search party had no choice but to go home and try again the next day.

The second day on the mountain came and went much the same as the first, but this time the sun was hotter, throats were drier, and tempers were shorter. Otto's shovel broke on a stubborn chunk of granite. Marco suffered a welt on his forehead when the shovel's splintered handle flew at him. By the end of the day, Rudi's fingers were scraped bloody, and he felt sick to his stomach. Otto was sure it was heat exhaustion. But Rudi knew otherwise.

Oma stood waiting for them at the village gates. Rudi could only shake his head.

Two days gone, and only one day left. One day to find the coin, or not. One day until Rudi's folly would doom the entire village to a fate he could hardly dare to imagine.

Meanwhile, the villagers had been busy collecting

their treasures and their loose change, and piling it into a chest at the mayor's house. He'd kept an accounting of every item deposited there, and by the end of the second day the town had collected coins and currency worth two thousand florins. There was also a pile of rings, chains, and medallions of various precious metals and undetermined value. As promised, there was the antique coin minted during the reign of King Balthazar the Elder (before he went mad). There was even one tiny gilt goblet, which was familiar to everyone, yet no one took credit for bringing it from its usual resting place. The mayor ordered it promptly returned to the church, with apologies to the good father, to be held in reserve for only the most desperate of needs.

And so by the end of that second day, the mayor estimated that the people of Brixen had collected perhaps four thousand florins' worth of coins, currency, and treasures.

Six thousand florins short of a golden guilder. And, Rudi knew, even six thousand florins more would not be enough.

CHAPTER 18

THE THIRD DAY. The final day.

Rudi dreaded going up the mountain, because he dreaded the thought of coming home without the golden guilder. But he had no choice.

Otto tried to recruit helpers from the village, but it was no use. Most of his neighbors were so intent on scraping together the fiddler's ransom, they would barely listen.

"No time for such foolishness," they said.

A few were willing to believe there might be a coin up the slope, but they would not place all their hope on the chance of finding one tiny trinket hidden somewhere on the mountain. They stayed at home to hunt for their own tiny trinkets: six thousand florins worth of copper and silver that might still be hiding in the back of cupboards and at the bottom of trunks.

As for Rudi, he was tempted to fill a knapsack with warm clothes and a hunk of cheese, so that if he should fail in his effort, he might turn his back on Brixen and never return. For what would there be to return home to, if the fiddler was not paid?

But all this was his own fault, Rudi reminded himself. Whether he found the coin or not, he must bear witness to whatever might come next.

What *would* come next? Rudi wondered as he trudged up the mountain. The rats might come back, perhaps in even greater numbers than before. Or it might be frogs, or milk blight, or who knows what kind of spiteful, devastating curse? Perhaps the witch's servant would simply take all their gathered gold and precious objects after all, rendering the entire village destitute for years to come. Rudi could not drive the worst possibilities out of his head.

If Marco and Otto shared his fears, they did not show it. Today they carried rakes and pitchforks, declaring that such implements were better suited to sifting through the piles of loose rock. Rudi's hands were swollen and sore, and he swore he knew the size and shape and color of every stone on the mountain.

Now, as he scooped up a handful of rocks, another possibility returned to Rudi's mind. Had someone else made off with the coin after all? Perhaps a foreign traveler had stumbled upon it and taken it home, only to subject his own village to locusts or hay rot or some such lamentable scourge. Perhaps a magpie had spied it from the air, snatched it up, and swallowed it.

But then, why would the witch send her servant to torment Brixen? Wouldn't she know better than anyone the whereabouts of her own coin?

A glimmer of an idea came to Rudi then, but it was lost just as quickly. For out of the corner of his eye, across the field of stones, Rudi saw a glint of sunlight on metal.

He scrambled toward it, and his heart fluttered in his chest. He tried not to hope that he had found the golden guilder at last. But hope came welling up his throat and out from his mouth: "I see something!"

Rudi heard Marco and Otto clambering toward him, but he dared not take his gaze off the glimmery spot, lest he lose it forever. A few more steps and he was upon it. He knelt down and reached for the object, which shone with the dark luster of tarnished metal—round and flat, and decidedly not a piece of the mountain.

Rudi grabbed the thing between finger and thumb, but it held fast. Then another gentle but persistent tug, and the object came free in Rudi's hand, flinging a shower of pebbles into the air as the mountain finally relinquished its grasp.

"What have you found?" said Marco, breathless from his running, or from his excitement, or both.

"Bless us!" gasped Otto, scrambling toward Rudi from the other direction. "Is it the coin at last? Shouldn't it be singing?"

A groan escaped Rudi's lips, and he sat down in a heap. Then, with great effort, as if the small object in his hand were made of lead, he held it up for the others to see.

For a moment there was nothing but black silence.

Otto took a step closer, bent over Rudi, and frowned.

"A spoon?" he said.

Marco's face became red as a foreboding sunset. "We've spent three days scraping in the dust and the dirt for a *spoon*?" He threw his rake across the field of stone, where it bounced with a clatter. "We're all idiots. Idiots!"

Rudi blinked in sour disappointment at the object in his hand. It was indeed a silver spoon. It was dented and flattened and tarnished nearly black from exposure to the weather, but still it glimmered softly in the waning light.

"This has been nothing but folly," spat Marco. "I'm going home." He marched to the spot where his rake had landed, snatched it up, and made for the clearing and the path into the forest.

Rudi did not try to stop him. Instead, he fervently wished he'd packed his hunk of cheese after all.

Otto pulled Rudi to his feet. "I'm sorry, lad. The light is fading, and the day is almost done." He took the spoon and pushed it deep into Rudi's coat pocket. Then he gathered his tools and tugged Rudi by the arm. Soon they were following Marco downslope and toward home.

"We should not despair," said Otto as they trounced downhill. "How does a sterling spoon come to be on the mountainside? I take it as a sign. It's not a golden guilder, but it must have some value. Perhaps considerable value. This may be our deliverance after all."

Neither Rudi nor Marco answered, but (if such a thing were possible) their silence became more thoughtful. At any rate, the urge Rudi felt to turn on his heels and run away faded ever so slightly. Otto might be right about the spoon. Rudi prayed he would be right.

But then came a sound, and Rudi stopped. "Do you hear that?"

Otto and Marco stopped too, and lifted their heads.

"I do," said Otto. "Is that a bird?"

It was so faint that the slightest wisp of air carried the sound away from their ears.

"I hear it too," said Marco. "It's not a bird. It sounds like someone whistling." He looked around for the source of the sound. But it was only the three of them.

Then Otto's eyes grew wide, and a grin spread across his face. "It's just as you said, Rudi. It must be the coin at last, wanting to be found."

CHAPTER 19

THEY STOOD still as rabbits, listening. Soon enough they heard it again, distant and wavering on the breeze.

"It's your singing coin!" said Otto. "Our deliverance has come at the eleventh hour!" He grasped Rudi by the shoulders and nearly kissed him. But then his brow furrowed. "My ears are playing tricks on me. The sound isn't coming from the field of rocks. Have we spent three days searching the wrong place?"

"My ears are playing the same tricks, then," said Marco. "I hear music coming from that way." He pointed downslope, and he was right. The music was growing louder now, and it was coming from below them on the path.

Now the sound filled Rudi's ears, and his knees

became weak under him as the truth dashed his last hopes. "That's not the coin." He closed his eyes and strained to hear, to be sure his ears were not deceived. "It sounds like a fiddle."

In a moment's time there could be no doubt. It was the fiddle, though its tune was nothing like before. The music it had played for the rats had been curious, and grating, and slightly off-key, as if a skilled musician was deliberately fingering the wrong strings. But now—now the music was perfectly in tune. It was joyful and mournful all at the same time, and despite himself, Rudi longed to hear it more clearly. He thought it might be the most beautiful music he'd ever heard.

Otto's smile faded, and he tilted his head. "The lad is right. That's fiddle music." He dropped his hands from Rudi's shoulders and stood, listening.

"Is that so?" said Marco, scowling. But then his brow smoothed, and his mouth fell open, and he listened too. Rudi was glad to have a moment longer to hear the music. A small part of him wished he could go on listening forever.

Then Marco blinked as if awakening from a dream. "The fiddler! What's that scoundrel up to now?" And he stomped off down the path.

Otto shook himself. "Perhaps he's making his

way back to Brixen," he said. "That means the time for reckoning is at hand! Hurry! We must add the spoon to the ransom. What if it makes all the difference?" And he hastened down the path after Marco.

Rudi's reverie was chased away by a sick feeling in the pit of his stomach. The spoon would not make any difference. Not a single treasure could make any difference, except the one that had not been found. Steeling himself for what awaited them in the village, he followed the others down the slope and toward the reckoning that had come at last.

"Wait!" All at once, Marco stopped and lifted a hand. Otto nearly collided with him, and Rudi nearly collided with Otto. "Listen. The music is getting louder. I think it's coming closer."

Otto's face lost all its color. "The fiddler is coming up the mountain. Has he already been to Brixen? Is the transaction finished, and we've missed it?"

"He's playing a happy enough tune," said Marco, uncertainty in his eyes. "Perhaps that's a good sign."

But Rudi knew in his heart that nothing they heard from the fiddler could be good. They hurried down the steep path toward the sound.

Then, when they were nearly out of the forest, the tune grew fainter. Instead of coming from the path below, now it seemed to be coming from somewhere off to the side, through the depths of the forest.

Suddenly, Rudi felt a strong urge to run off once more. It was not fear of returning home, though he still felt that keenly. It was something else: more like he was being drawn *toward* something, rather than being driven *away* from something.

It was the music. Faint as it was, the fiddler's music once again became irresistible to Rudi. He needed to hear it more clearly, and just now nothing was more important. Without a word, without a thought, Rudi turned off the path and began crashing through the ferns and underbrush, in the direction of the music.

"What do you think you're doing?" said Marco. "You'll not run off to chase any music. You'll come with us to face the music that's waiting at home!" And he plowed through the thicket, grabbed Rudi by the arm, and steered him back onto the path.

"But the fiddler!" cried Rudi. "Otto is right! He's already been to Brixen, I know it. He's going back up the mountain to join the witch." And he tried to pull away.

"Good riddance to him, then," thundered Marco, tightening his grip on Rudi's arm. "Either they've paid him enough or they haven't, and there's nothing we can do about it now. Besides, what more can he do to us? Send rats again? We'll be

131

ready for him this time. Whatever scourge he wants to bring upon us, let him try. He can't harm us any more than he already has."

Rudi wished he could be so sure. He was sure of only one thing. "I must go!" he protested, and he yanked his arm, but the blacksmith's grip was tight. They continued at pace down the mountain.

Rudi could not understand his own longing to seek out the fiddler. The thought of seeing the witch's servant terrified Rudi, and it repulsed him.

It was the music. Some deep, stubborn part of Rudi could not resist it. He yearned to hear this music as he'd never yearned for anything before. It made him want to dance and shout and weep, all at the same time. "A trick," he told himself, and yet if Marco had loosened his grasp even the slightest bit, Rudi would have run off and never looked back.

But Marco did not loosen his grasp.

Before long they were trooping across the near meadow, within sight of the village. With each step downslope, the tune grew fainter, as did Rudi's urge to follow it. So quickly did the melody fade from his memory that within a few moments Rudi wondered why he'd ever had such a desire to hear it in the first place.

Dusk was falling, but Rudi did not see the expected glow of lamplight from the houses below.

With every step homeward the sky grew darker, yet no new light sprang from any window. By the time they crossed the footbridge that marked the edge of Brixen, it was near full dark, and still the village had not gone about its usual routine.

Then a light sprang up from somewhere between the houses.

"They've gathered in the square," said Marco. Still pulling Rudi, and with Otto following, he made for the village center. As they approached, the glow became brighter, and now they could hear voices. They made their way through the lanes and alleyways, until the cobbles and buildings glowed orange from reflected firelight.

Was there a bonfire in the square? Rudi could not imagine why. And the voices now were louder, and more strident. He thought he heard sobbing.

They turned the last corner and into the square.

It was a madhouse of frantic activity. A mob of men had gathered near the fountain, and the torches they carried cast frightening red shadows across their faces. Women stood in clusters, falling against each other, sobbing, wailing as if their very souls had been torn from their bodies. And the children . . .

"Where are all the other children?" said Rudi.

CHAPTER 20

RUDI'S EYES scoured the square for his friends—for a glimpse of Konrad or Nicolas, or Roger, or Susannah Louisa. But there was no one close to his own age. He prayed the other children were hiding, or had been told to stay at home, but he knew neither could be true. The children of Brixen had never been banished from the village square, for any reason. The square belonged to Rudi and all his friends. It was their playground and their sanctuary, and by rights they were allowed to participate in anything that happened here. They had witnessed Herbert Wenzel tallying his rats; they had watched the fiddler as he led the remaining rats out of town. The square was the children's domain as surely as Marco had his forge or Otto his bakery or Rudi's father his dairy. Seeing none of his friends now, anywhere, left Rudi's mouth dry and his heart fluttering wildly in his chest.

Marco had found the mayor in the milling crowd and was interrogating him. Rudi could make out only a few words above the din of voices, but the mayor's frantic gestures told the tale: "Would not take the payment (*shaking head*). . . . Spilled it to the floor (*spreading arms wide*). . . . He went that way (*pointing*). . . . The fiddle (*one arm sawing across the other*) . . . the children . . . Gone!"

There could be no mistaking the mayor's last word. *Gone.* All the children of Brixen, except Rudi. And the fiddler had led them away.

Rudi needed to hear every word for himself. He stepped closer, but for the second time that day, someone pulled at his arm.

It was Oma. "Come with me." She led him to a quiet lane around a corner.

Rudi grasped her thin shoulders as if they were a lifeline. "Where are they? What has he done with them?"

But he already knew the answer. They had followed the music. That was why it had enticed him so when he'd heard it on the mountain: It had been meant to entice him.

Oma gazed at him with a steady sorrow, but she said nothing.

Rudi made an effort to calm himself. To think clearly. "He took them up the mountain. I heard him, Oma. We must go find them!"

Oma shook her head. "Not until first light. You'll only thrash around and get lost up there in the dark. The men know that here"—she tapped her own forehead—"but still they light their torches. It makes them feel like they're doing something, when at the moment there's nothing to be done."

"Oma," said Rudi in a voice barely above a whisper. "All this for one coin?"

She sighed. "I don't suppose you found it up there today?"

"No." Then he asked her. "All of them, Oma? All . . . but me?"

Oma patted his cheek, and her face was stoic as always, but her eyes were brimming. "As easily as if they were rats. The music—" She caught her breath. "Never in my life have I heard such music. I admit I stood transfixed. We all did. All except the children. The older ones plucked the babies from their mothers' arms, and off they went, every last one, as happily as if they'd been waiting for this day their entire lives."

Rudi knew what she was speaking of. The music had been achingly beautiful. Mesmerizing. He suddenly realized that he'd been lucky. Lucky that Marco and Otto had been only briefly transfixed by the music. Lucky that they'd pulled him back instead of letting him run off after the fiddler.

But Rudi wasn't sure he wanted to be lucky if it meant also being heartbroken.

From around the corner came a continuing flurry of arguments, sobs, and lamentations. Oma sighed, and for the first time in his life, Rudi thought she looked truly old.

She continued. "For three days they piled up everything they owned: wedding rings, bits of heirloom silver, every last penny they could find." Then Oma wrinkled her nose as if she had tasted something sour. "But *he* scoffed at it all, and then he railed when the coin was nowhere in the hoard. It sent chills through me such as I've never felt in all my life. That servant of the witch's—he'd be emissary to the Devil himself, if only the Devil would have him."

"The witch is punishing us, and it's all my fault," said Rudi.

He thought about his friends, envisioning each face in turn: Konrad and Roger and all the scruffy boys. Nicolas, who liked to brag and boast. Greta and Johanna and every silly little girl. Marta, with the lovely eyes. The collection of chubby babies, whose names he could not keep straight. Susanna Louisa. He imagined them following the fiddler happily, willingly, joyfully even. What were they doing now, on the dark, cold mountain, with no bewitching music playing in their ears to distract them? Who would give them their supper and put the little ones to bed?

All for a coin. All because he had found a coin, and lost the coin, and failed to find the coin again. Rudi shivered, and he drew his coat tighter around himself. That's when he felt the lump in his pocket.

He pulled out the spoon and turned it over in the flickering firelight. Absently he said, "I found this. . . ."

Oma drew in a sharp breath and snatched the spoon. "Where?"

"On the mountain. In the place I thought the coin would be." He studied Oma's face. "What does it mean?"

"I need to think about that." She held the spoon close to her face and inspected it in the dim light. "But things are beginning to make sense."

"They are?" For, truly, Rudi was so wracked with guilt and grief that he could make sense of nothing.

"Perhaps . . . ," she said, and then she looked at him. "Perhaps you did not find the coin on the mountain because the coin was not there after all."

Rudi's heart sank. "How will we get everyone back without the coin? I must find that coin!"

Then he stopped, and forced himself to think. "But I need to go with the search party. I heard the music too, Oma. Perhaps I can remember which way the fiddler went."

For a moment Oma frowned in thought. "No," she said decisively, and gave him back the spoon. "Otto and Marco can go with the search party. You will deliver this to the witch. And you will tell her what happened, and she will tell you what you must do to get our children back."

CHAPTER 21

EARLY THE next morning, Rudi found himself climbing the mountain once more.

He accompanied the search party as far as the forest, to the spot where the music had faded the day before. Here they stopped, and Marco and Otto prepared to lead a dozen men through the underbrush, in the direction the music had gone. They carried knives and slingshots and pitchforks. They carried knapsacks filled with buttered bread, and skins filled with water. They carried coats for their children, who had run off without them, and who would be shivering by the time they were found.

For the children had to be found.

Otto placed a hand on Rudi's shoulder. "Are you sure you don't want company? We could spare a man or two, I'm sure."

"No," said Rudi, though he did not look forward to making his journey alone. But he alone had caused the trouble in the first place. He alone must make things right. "I know the way. Besides, you might need every man you've got."

Otto nodded and shook Rudi's hand. "May we meet again soon. We'll mark our trail." He made good his word by pulling a scrap of cloth from a small sack and tying it onto the nearest low-hanging branch.

"Let's get moving, then," came Marco's voice from the front of the group. "Good luck to you, lad. I hope you know what you're doing."

Rudi waved to Marco. He hoped so too.

He continued on up the path alone, with the morning sun already hot on his back and the mountain wind brisk on his cheeks. It had been months since he'd first stumbled upon the mouth of the cave, and on that day the sleet and snow had nearly blinded him. But he felt sure that today he would choose the right path.

He'd had a strange conversation with Oma last night, after everyone had gone home to fitful, mournful sleep. For how can parents sleep in a house that's suddenly empty of their children's breathing? But the children could not be saved by parents who were too exhausted to think clearly, or to pack a few days' worth of food, or to climb the Berg in search of their dear ones. And so Brixen had slept, but restlessly, and for only a few hours.

Satisfied that Rudi's own parents were finally asleep, Oma had rocked in her chair and told Rudi this: The spoon belonged to the witch and needed to be returned to her.

Rudi sat up with a start. "How do you know it's hers?"

She shook her head. "It's bad luck to talk of such things. But you will take it to her. And you will ask her about the coin. There must be a reason you found that spoon in the same place the coin was lost."

Rudi inspected the spoon again in the light of the hearth. It looked ordinary enough. Silver, yes, and with a twisted handle, but it would not have been out of place on any supper table in Brixen. And it was pitted and dented and badly tarnished.

"Did she find the coin? Is that why I couldn't find it?"

Oma rocked harder. "I cannot say for certain. But still I feel that something is not right. First rats. And now this horrible business, stealing innocent children. Our witch is powerful, and she can be angered, but she's not cruel."

"Her servant is much more powerful than we thought," Rudi said. "How can such a thing happen?"

Oma stared into the fire. "It seems the witch has cause to mistrust her servant as much as we do. Go up and tell her what's happened. Ask her what you can do about it. There is no hope for getting your friends back unless you beg the help of the witch."

Now, as Rudi climbed, questions swirled in his mind. How did Oma know the spoon belonged to the witch? And why would the witch allow her servant to wield such power? Once again, he was left to think that Oma knew much more than she was willing to tell.

Rudi climbed higher, always keeping to the path, no matter how much it meandered and twisted. This time he would take no shortcuts. Recalling his three days of futile searching, he could not even cast a glance at the field of scree as he passed it.

He wondered if he was doing the right thing. What kind of fool seeks out the witch in her own country? Why would the witch even want to help him, when he'd already caused her so much trouble? She'd take one look at him and strike him with a bolt of lightning. Or turn him into a rat, or worse. But he couldn't think of anything worse. Still he kept on, for the sake of all his friends. If Oma said this was the only way, then it must be so.

Rudi climbed, and the sun climbed higher in the sky. Summer was fleeting on the Berg. Even now, on a mid-July day, the air on the slope of the mountain was cool. In a few weeks' time the frosts and snows would return, and already Rudi could feel winter's promise in the chilly air.

Before long, he found himself at an outcropping of rock that looked to all the world like a huge stone bench.

"The Witch's Chair!" Rudi knew that's what it must be, though he hadn't seen it last October, when he'd first stumbled upon the coin. Perhaps the sleet had obscured it from his view then, for today some inner compass told him this was the right way.

Rudi thought how much fun he'd have telling Susanna Louisa that the Witch's Chair was real after all, and that he had seen it with his own eyes, and sat upon it himself. Then his throat grew tight and his eyes burned. What if he never had the chance to tell Susanna Louisa?

Where were the other children now? Had they

survived the cold night on the mountain while Rudi himself had enjoyed the refuge of his hearth? He'd slept not a wink; still, he'd been warm and safe. But his friends—Rudi could hardly bear to think of what his friends were going through.

He had to find the way to the witch's cave. He had to endure whatever horrible things the witch might do, and plead for her help in returning all the children of Brixen to their homes and families. It was the only way.

Now he came upon a huge crack in the mountain; one of its many jagged peaks was broken in half from top to bottom by some violent force long past. The crack was just wide enough for a man to step through. Or a boy. Or a witch.

Rudi advanced toward the crevice and stepped inside, where he was engulfed in chilly shadow. Sheer rock loomed on either side of him, so high that he could not see the top of either rock face. He was sure this crevice had been here for immeasurable eons, and would most likely remain here for immeasurable eons more. But he could not push from his mind the image of something—or someone—swooping down to slam the two halves together and obliterate him forever like two hands crushing a bug.

Rudi shuddered. He was about to bolt out the other side of the crevice and into the blinding sunlight, when he stopped. He stood in the shadow and blinked until his eyes became accustomed to the dim light. And that is when he saw the opening in the rock, barely as high as his waist. He knelt down and peered inside.

"I've found it," he said to himself. "I've found the entrance to the witch's lair."

Then, before he could think another thought, an arm reached out from the darkness, grabbed him by the collar, and yanked him inside.

CHAPTER 22

A DARK FIGURE loomed over him. A blast of
cold air swirled at him, and Rudi gasped at its
sharpness. The figure stood between him and the
entrance, so that Rudi could see only a black and
faceless silhouette against the daylight. It reached
down toward him.

Rudi fumbled at his belt, trying to find his knife,
but then he stopped.

It was only a hand extended toward him, waiting.
The frail-looking hand of someone very old and
very small.

Instinctively, Rudi grasped it, and it pulled him
to his feet with surprising strength. Then the
figure brushed past him and disappeared into the
darkness of the cave.

For a moment Rudi stood frozen in fear, but then

he forced himself to follow. After all, this was why he had come.

There came another gust of wind, and behind him the door slammed shut, sealing them inside the mountain. Instantly the cold wind ceased, and they were left in a blackness that softened to dim candlelight.

"You again!" said a voice. "You've already caused me all manner of trouble."

Rudi opened his mouth, ready to protest or to beg for mercy. But the figure turned its back without waiting for a reply.

It busied itself with something in a dark corner. Presently, the dark corner sprang to light as a pile of embers glowed and then licked at a small log. The firelight revealed a furnished room: a braided rug, a cushioned armchair, a sturdy wooden table, a low footstool.

The figure straightened and brushed its hands together. It took off its cloak, hung it on a peg, and turned to face Rudi.

She was nothing but an old woman. Much older than Oma. Perhaps no taller than Susanna Louisa. Her white hair was tucked under a ragged kerchief, and her apron was threadbare. A thousand lines creased her face, but her back was straight and her step was quick.

Rudi gulped down his fear. "You—you can't be the Brixen Witch."

"Why not?"

"Because," said Rudi, "the Brixen Witch is fearsome. She's terrible to look at, with teeth like spikes and foul, icy breath."

"Ha!" she said. "I has no need for such display. I believe you has something of mine?" She held out her hand.

For a moment Rudi frowned in puzzlement. Then, "Oh!" He reached into his pocket and produced the silver spoon.

She polished it with her apron. "What else have you brought? Most people who comes to see the witch brings gifts. Offerings. Supplication."

Rudi blinked, and he patted his pockets. Finally, he brought out a small package and unwrapped it. "My grandmother packed provisions. You're welcome to them." For though she didn't look fearsome, Rudi decided it would be best to make the witch happy.

She peeked into the cloth and nodded with satisfaction. "Ahh, elderberry tarts. Lovely. I accept your gift."

Rudi decided to ask before he lost his courage.

"Do you have the golden guilder?"

She shook the spoon at him. "Smart lad."

"Did you dig it up with that?"

She regarded the spoon, frowning. "'Twas handy at the time. One cannot spend precious minutes rummaging for a garden spade at a time like that. One is likely to miss the opportunity altogether. And that would be bad. Very bad."

Sliding into the armchair, she pointed at the footstool. "I regret I has no other chair to offer. 'Tis not often I have visitors who stay."

"I don't mind." Rudi sat on the stool, and his knees nearly touched his chin. The fire gave off a cheerful glow, and it was already chasing the dampness from the cave. Rudi found himself thinking that this was quite a homey place, for a cave. But he remained wary. She was a witch, after all.

"So," said the witch, sitting back and resting her hands on her chest. "Young Rudolf Augustin Bauer."

Rudi's mouth fell open. "How do you—"

"The family resemblance is unmistakable," she said. "Rudolf is your Christian name, but no one calls you that."

He shook his head. "Rudi," he squeaked.

"Ah, yes. Rudi." Her eyes bore into him. "What kind of name is that for a boy?"

Rudi could only shrug. "Rudolf Augustin is a

family name. Papa said I'd grow into it, but Oma—
my grandmother—said it was too big a name for a
newborn child. She called me Rudi, and it stuck."
He sat up as tall as he could manage while sitting
so low to the ground. "I *have* grown since then."

"Quite," said the witch. "But still you're called
Rudi. Methinks old habits die hard. Anyway, I like
it. It suits you. How is your grandmother?"

"Very well, thank you, mistress," Rudi croaked
out of habit. But then his mouth dropped open
again. "You—know my grandmother?"

So this was why Oma seemed to know so much!
This was how she'd seen the spoon before.

"Aye, Gussie is a lovely girl, and well spoken.
Though I suppose she's not a girl any longer if
she's become a grandmother. I see she's learned
not to burn the elderberry tarts." The witch took a
satisfied bite.

A thousand questions swirled in Rudi's head.
"How did you know I had your spoon?"

She sniffed. "I'm the witch of this mountain. It's
my business to know where mine own things are."

"That's how you found the coin as well?"

She nodded.

Then a thought occurred to Rudi, and another
piece of the puzzle fell into place. "You found
the coin last spring, didn't you? That's why my
nightmares stopped."

"Aye."

"But I lost it last October. Why did you take so long to retrieve it if you knew where it was?" And my nightmares could have stopped that much sooner, Rudi thought, but he held his tongue.

"The snows came, firstly."

Rudi knew she spoke the truth. He remembered how the very day after he'd lost the coin in the avalanche, winter's first snow had fallen. If not for that, he would have gone up to unbury it himself, in an effort to banish the nightmares.

"Though, truthfully, a mere few feet of snow are not a burden to me." Now the witch shifted uncomfortably in her chair. "There were other . . . impediments. I could not go straightaway. But the first chance I got, that's what I did. I ventured down and dug up the coin, before anyone else could." She cast a furtive glance behind her, as if expecting something to jump out of the shadows. But nothing moved except the tongues of flame in the grate.

Another question burned in Rudi's mind. "Did you send the rats?"

"Rats?" She shuddered. "Never. Why would I, anyway, once I found my coin?"

"You wouldn't," said Rudi, thinking out loud. "No more torment once the coin was returned to its rightful owner." And then he remembered again what Herbert Wenzel had said: that the rats could not be the witch's doing. That the witch's hexes were more . . . poetical.

"I regret I could not intervene in that nasty business," she continued. "I've been . . . indisposed these past months." Again she stirred in her chair, and Rudi sensed she was not telling him everything.

But a different question leapt from his tongue—a question he was sure he knew the answer to. "Your servant sent the rats, didn't he?"

The witch's eyes blazed, and she drew her hands into fists. "Him! Day after day he sits in some corner, sharpening his teeth. As if he weren't ugly enough."

Rudi shivered.

She scowled. "Aye, he's the one sent the rats. He steals from me too. He tried to steal the coin one day, but he dropped it just outside my door. And then some child stumbled upon it and carried it away." The witch cast a sharp eye at Rudi.

Rudi gulped as he remembered that day. One simple act had set all the past months' troubles into motion.

Other thoughts crowded into Rudi's head. "Your servant has betrayed you, then."

The witch sighed in anger and frustration. "And now I'm all but prisoner here inside this mountain. I risked my life to collect that coin, mind you. I waited for the snows to melt, and then I waited till he was off on some vile errand. Gone to curdle the cream in Petz, or some such." She held up the tarnished spoon. "I took what was at hand, and at dusk I stole out. I was back again before he knew I was gone. If he had found me out, that would've been the end of me. He's grown powerful enough."

Rudi tried to understand all that he'd heard. "It's only one small coin. Why does he want it so badly? And why did you risk your life for it?"

She growled under her breath. "He's been stealing my magic. Little by little, over many years. I hides it, here and there, within unassuming objects: a coil of rope, a cracked teapot. Buried with the potatoes in my garden. In the hollow of that old fiddle that sat in the corner for ages. I thought he could not find the magic, or if he could, it would be only small kernels here and there. But he's clever, is that one. Piece by piece, he found my magic and stole it away. All but this." The witch carefully drew something from her apron pocket.

The golden guilder. She held it up, and it shimmered in the firelight. Its ancient markings were visible to Rudi even from a distance.

"This holds nearly all that remains of my magic. If he takes possession of this coin, all will be lost. I will be nothing but an old woman several hundred years old. And he will be all powerful. You've seen what he's like. Such a thing would be bad. Very bad."

Rudi sat frozen. No wonder the fiddler had caused so much sorrow and grief. But the witch was wrong about one thing: Things were already very bad.

"He doesn't know you have the coin," said Rudi. "He thinks it's still in Brixen."

She nodded. "'Tis why he sent the rats. I told you already, I could not intervene. I hasn't done my duty as your witch, and for that I'm truly anguished. But I seems to be stuck here."

Rudi cleared his throat. "Yes, mistress, but don't you know there's new trouble now? And it's far worse than the rats." Rudi took a breath and blurted out his sorrowful message. "He's stolen all the children from Brixen."

"He's *what*?" She jumped out of her chair in alarm. Despite her clear distress, it occurred to Rudi that this was less dramatic than it might have been, since she was no taller standing than she'd been while sitting.

"It's true," said Rudi. "He led them away, and up the mountain. Every one of them, except me. I thought you said you knew everything?"

Now she wheeled upon him, and the fire flared in the grate, and Rudi was fervently sorry he had ever doubted her fearsomeness. "I said I know where *my* things are. Not *every* thing." She turned and began to pace the floor. "I've been such a fool! What is that fiend up to now?"

Rudi fought to swallow his own grief and fear. And though hope was vanishing like a meadow under snow, he knew that he must somehow do what he had come to do.

"Pardon, mistress, but I came to beg your help."

"Help?" cried the witch. Once more the fire flared, and now the mountain rumbled around them. If this was all the magic she had left, Rudi wondered, how terrible would she be with all her power? "I'm stuck, I tell you! Near powerless. I'm afeared to go to sleep, lest he sneak in here and take the coin from me. And you asks me to help you? Here's what I'd like to know: Who's going to help *me*?"

CHAPTER 23

RUDI STARED at her, feeling as if he'd been slapped. How had he ever thought it would be a good idea to visit the witch?

Oma had sent him. She had told Rudi this would be his only chance to find the other children. Because Oma knew much more than she had ever told him. Because Oma herself had met the witch.

But that had been long ago, and many things had changed since then. The witch could not help him now.

What had he expected, anyway? That the witch would flick her wrist, and all his friends would magically appear?

Well . . . yes. Something like that.

The witch paced the floor of her cave, muttering to herself and pulling at strands of hair. She tossed a log onto the fire, sending a burst of red embers up the chimney.

"You have been nothing but bad luck," she said. "And now here you are in mine own house, bringing more trouble with you."

Rudi stiffened. The witch was right, of course, strictly speaking. Simply by picking up a coin, he had set off a series of disasters, finally bringing his entire village, and now the witch herself, to the limits of despair.

But was it truly bad luck? Or was it only a matter of how you looked at things?

"If you please, mistress," said Rudi to the witch. "It's true I had a hand in causing the trouble. But what would have happened had I *not* picked up the golden guilder outside your door? If not for me, your servant might have picked up the coin himself. And then what? You'd be in much bigger trouble than you are now. We all would be." Rudi eyed her nervously. Was he foolish to argue with a witch?

She pointed a finger at him. "You only managed to lose the coin again. Falling on the loose rock, causing an avalanche. I risked everything going out to find it, digging in piles of nasty sharp rock with nothing but a spoon."

Rudi stood and shook out the cramps in his legs. He might be foolish to argue with a witch, but somehow he'd feel like a bigger fool if he did not. "At least your servant could not find it. No one but yourself could find it. You might even say I hid it for you." *Accidentally*, thought Rudi, *but nevertheless*.

"You hid it, true enough," said the witch, stepping closer. "You spent three days on this mountain and could not find it."

"Because it wasn't there!" said Rudi, and the witch scowled at him.

"Besides," he continued, growing bolder, "if not for that, I would have been in Brixen when the fiddler came back. I would be with all the other children now, waiting to be rescued, instead of here."

"Aye, here," she scoffed. "And what use are you here, might I ask? Bringing me elderberry tarts, and bad news to wash them down with."

Rudi's jaw clenched, and his hands balled into fists. He had endured too much in the past months to allow anyone to scoff at him. Even a witch. His heart thumped in his chest and his mouth went dry, but he bent toward her until their noses nearly touched. "If you please, mistress. You want me on your side. I was the one who worked alongside Herbert Wenzel, catching rats, when no one else had the stomach for it. I was the one to stand up in the village hall and make the bargain with the fiddler. I knew what he wanted, even when no one else would listen. *I*. Me. Rudolf Augustin Bauer."

Rudi supposed she might use her remaining magic to turn him into a bug. But he didn't care. He was tired of hearing about bad luck, tired of *being* bad luck. It was time to make his own luck.

The witch did not turn him into a bug. She only sighed and slumped into her chair.

Rudi gulped. Perhaps he had been too bold. "I'm sorry for all that's happened. Truly I am. But your troubles and my troubles seem to have the same cause. Perhaps there is a way we can help each other."

She narrowed her eyes at him. "And how shall we do that? What do you think I've been doing these last months, locked inside this mountain? Knitting socks? I've done nothing else but think about such things." She shook her head, and now she spoke barely above a whisper. "I has no solution. And now I fear it's too late."

Sorrow and frustration crept across her face. Rudi wondered if witches ever wept, and worried that he might soon find out. He decided he liked her better when she was irritable.

"Please, mistress," he tried again. "You are the witch of this mountain. You don't mean to let your servant defeat you?"

The witch blinked, and then looked up at him, as if seeing him for the first time. "Shame on me.

Gussie sends me her very own grandson, and how does I repay the favor? Here he is, just a snippet of a lad, cheeks as soft as a lamb's ears, and he speaks more sense than my own self." She stood, grabbed Rudi's head, pulled it toward her own, and kissed him on both cheeks. "I'm glad you've come, Rudolf Augustin Bauer."

Rudi's face grew hot, but his heart leapt. "Thank you, mistress."

Then her eyes flared, and she began her pacing once more. "I *am* the witch of this mountain. He is nothing but an impostor. A thief and a fraud. As long as I have one scrap of magic remaining, I shall not give over my realm to *him*."

Again there came a low rumble all around them, as if the mountain were a watchdog growling under its breath.

"Tell me what I can do, mistress, and I'll do it," said Rudi.

"Aye," she said, almost to herself. "We needs a plan. He's sly, is that one, but he has weaknesses. Boundless greed, for one thing. What else?" Now she turned and faced Rudi, and he wasn't sure if she was testing him or if she truly wanted to know.

"Well. . . ." Rudi thought of the fiddler, with his wild hair, and icy breath, and shirt of motley patches. He could have set mosquitoes upon Brixen to punish them, or rain, but instead he chose rats.

He could have lured the children away with sweets, or with stories, but instead he flourished a fiddle. How different he was from the witch, who did not brandish her power with arrogance.

"He likes to show off," said Rudi.

The witch squinted at Rudi, and a hint of a grin flashed across her face. "Clever lad." She pulled the golden guilder from her pocket and held it up to the firelight. "So. Greed and vanity. For this prize he'll do nearly anything, and all the better if he can make a show of it."

She pocketed the coin, satisfied. Then she turned and took a crockery teapot from a shelf. She pulled a handful of dried leaves from a bunch hanging on a peg and dropped them into the pot. "Sit. I'll brew us some tea."

Rudi blinked when the witch uttered the word "brew." But it was only tea, he told himself. No one ever called it "witch's tea." This must be perfectly safe, and besides, they were allies now. Weren't they?

As if to reassure Rudi, the witch muttered "ahh, chamomile" as she poured water from a steaming kettle into the teapot.

Rudi remained standing. "Excuse me, mistress, but shouldn't we go find my friends? Or do . . . something?"

She set the kettle onto the hearth with a clank.

"Where shall we find them? And how shall we get them out from under *his* watchful eye? Does you have a plan all formulated in your noggin already?"

Rudi sighed and shook his head. He had no plan. No idea at all.

CHAPTER 24

THE WITCH handed Rudi a crockery mug and a spoon. "Drink some tea. It will settle your stomach and help you think."

Rudi swallowed his frustration and stirred his tea. The spoon was silver, and it had a twisted handle. "This is how Oma knew the spoon was yours."

The witch grinned. "We did have tea, Gussie and I. And we shared her elderberry tarts. That reminds me. . . ." She rummaged among the things on her little table and produced the package Rudi had given her. "Have one."

Rudi thanked her and took one of Oma's tarts. It seemed there was nothing else he could do for the moment.

The witch settled into her chair with her own

mug of tea. "I knows him," she said, and Rudi knew she meant her servant. "He cannot abide children. He'll want to be rid of them quick enough." She took a bite of tart and grinned. "Ahh. Sixty years since I last tasted these. Have another."

Rudi shook his head. He wasn't feeling very hungry. "Rid of them? You don't think he's . . . gotten rid of them . . . already?"

"Oh, no," said the witch, brushing crumbs from her lap. "Those children are safe as can be. They're pawns, you know. He'll need to offer them in exchange for the coin."

"But we can never let him have the coin!"

"I should say not." She took another bite of tart.

Rudi struggled to keep his voice calm. "Then how are we going to get them back?"

"We'll have to think of something," said the witch. She sipped her tea.

Now Rudi squirmed on the footstool. He found no comfort in this conversation.

The witch set down her mug. "We are a formidable team, you has convinced me. Gussie's grandson and the Brixen Witch. But we needs a sound plan, and I always find that sound plans take a bit of rumination. We may have only one chance, and haste is our enemy. So now, tell me news of Gussie. She's feisty as ever, I hope?"

Rudi rubbed his forehead. He wanted to protest

that he was not good at ruminating, but she was smiling at him expectantly, and now she looked like nothing more than a frail old woman hungry for news of a long-lost friend.

He sighed. "Feisty? I suppose so. Though Papa says she's ornery, and Mama calls her prickly, and most of the villagers are just plain scared of her."

The witch sat back, satisfied. "That's the Gussie I remember."

"She's told me stories about you, but she never told me that she'd actually *met* you." Once more, Rudi thought that Oma had kept too much from him.

"Ah, well," said the witch. "'Tis bad luck to talk of such things."

Rudi sat up straight. "That's what Oma always says!"

The witch shook half a tart at him. "She's right. What would happen once such a thing became common knowledge? You'd be hounded night and day. People would be full of questions, begging you to intervene with the witch for them. Or worse—they'd look at you sidelong, thinking you've become a witch yourself, now that you've mingled with witchy folk." She shook her head. "No, one doesn't talk of visiting the witch. You'll see for yourself when you gets back."

If I get back, thought Rudi, but then another

question came to him. "Is Oma the only person in Brixen who's met you?"

The witch picked up her mug and blew on her tea. "Anymore. There were others before her, but now they're gone. 'Tis a good thing you ventured up, crisis or no. Someone needs to carry on the knowledge in that village."

"You mean me?" squeaked Rudi.

The witch shrugged. "It seems fitting. You are here. You are Gussie's grandson. You're not as feisty as she is, but you'll do."

Rudi couldn't argue with any of that. Still, he did not feel equal to the challenge.

"So," she continued, "it seems you're appointed to carry on the knowledge in the village. If you tells me what you already knows about the witch, I can tell you what you doesn't know."

Rudi hesitated. He wasn't sure he wanted to be the person to carry on the knowledge in the village. He wasn't sure he wanted the responsibility.

Then again, why not? Hadn't he just bragged to the witch about how capable he was? Catching rats, and making bargains with her servant, and now venturing up here alone. Why shouldn't he be the one to carry on Oma's task? In fact, now that he thought about it, Rudi decided he'd be proud to do it.

He tried to think. What did he know? He blurted

out the first thing that came into his mind.

"You're not as fearsome as I expected. But sometimes you do fearsome things."

The witch set her cup on the wooden table and folded her hands on her chest. "What sorts of things?"

Rudi played with his spoon. "Last year one of our cows birthed a stillborn calf. Mama said we'd angered you somehow, and so you cursed the cow and killed the calf." He sipped his tea and kept his eyes on the witch.

"Hmm," she said. "What do you suppose I was angry about?"

Rudi shrugged. "Mama said we should have done something more, once the cow was near her time. We did set out a pitcher of cream, and you took it, but Mama said it wasn't enough."

The witch sat back, thoughtful. "Ah, the cream. That were right nice. I hasn't got room up here for a cow. I remembers that birthing too. I heard the cow in the barn, lowing peculiar-like. Her calf was past help, poor thing. But 'twas nature's doing, not my own. I gave comfort to the mother, lest her milk seize up, but that's all. 'Twas not even magic. 'Twas only . . . a small kindness. A thank-you for the cream."

Such an explanation made sense to Rudi, and so he tried again.

"In Brixen, people say you send the storms. They say you send three ravens to circle the clock tower, and soon afterward, lightning strikes."

She raised an eyebrow. "I'm no fool. I knows enough to stay indoors when a storm is brewing. 'Tis more than I can say for some silly folk. To see storm clouds gathering is not sign enough for them. They needs to see the witch's signs before they come to their senses and run inside." She shook her head and *tsk*ed, the way Mama did whenever Rudi did something particularly childish.

He scratched his head. "Why do you bother, if we're such silly folk?"

"What kind of witch would I be otherwise? Brixen is under my charge, and Klausen, and all the villages hereabouts. 'Tis my duty. 'Tis the way it's always been. You may not think so, but you needs your witch."

"Sounds like you're just a midwife, really. Or a philosopher. Not really a witch," said Rudi, before he had a chance to think.

Now the witch leaned forward in her chair, and the fire flared in the grate. "You think the Brixen Witch is nothing but a little old woman who drinks chamomile tea and takes pity on suffering milk cows? Foolish child! I'll send a storm if it's called for, the likes of which would make you shake in your little farmer's boots." Then she sighed. "Or, at least, once upon a time I could."

Rudi was beginning to understand. The witch was part of the mountain, and a part of Brixen. She presided over their lives just as certainly as did the snows in winter and the sun in summer. Without the witch, the earth might just as well wobble off its axis onto a new—and disastrous—course.

He decided the time for rumination was done.

"There's a search party," he told her. "A dozen strong men, here on the mountain. Perhaps they can help retrieve your magic."

"Aye, I can hear them stomping about out there."

Rudi blinked at her. He strained to listen, but he heard only the crackling of the fire.

She sniffed. "You cannot hear them. This is my mountain. I can hear my own mountain breathe if I listens close enough. 'Tis like music to me."

And then a thought sprang into Rudi's head, and with it came a flood of hope.

"That's the answer," said Rudi. "That is how we can defeat him."

CHAPTER 25

A GIDDY excitement welled up in Rudi's chest. The idea seemed so simple. So perfect. And it had taken only one word.

"Music," he said. "We can defeat him with music."

The witch squinted at him. "Explain yourself, lad."

"You enchanted the golden guilder once, to make it sing. So your servant could find it, yes?"

"So *I* could find it," she said. "But I gave it a tuneless, maddening song. So's he would be repelled by it, despite its power. So that even though he chased you down the mountain and watched you all night, he could not abide touching the coin. Do you think a mere windowpane would be enough to keep him out of your house?"

Rudi swallowed a huge lump as he recalled that

171

first night, with the golden guilder buried in his trunk and his dear Papa leaning out into the storm, half-asleep. How near had they come to falling into the clutches of the evil servant that very first night? Rudi shuddered to think of it. But he pushed it out of his mind. "No matter," he told the witch, shaking himself. "It worked. The music had a powerful effect on him, did it not?"

The witch nodded. "That it did. Go on, then."

Rudi tried to organize his thoughts. "Later, he played your fiddle—the one with a bit of magic hidden inside. To lead away the rats, and then the children."

"I thought I heard music of some sort." She narrowed her eyes. "Did he play it well? Having the magic in one's possession is one thing. Knowing how to use it is something else."

Rudi hesitated. But he decided that the witch wanted to know the truth. "Yes, mistress. He played it very well."

"Bah!" she spat. "'Tis no great trick. Any fool with that much magic at his disposal could do such a thing." Now she shook her finger, and her eyes gleamed. "If I possessed all my magic, I'd have no need for a fiddle. I could make the plainest object sing so pure and clear, the nightingale would hide in shame."

"I've no doubt, mistress," said Rudi, though his

heart ached. He wished he could pledge to bring back every scrap of her magic, rescue his friends, and make safe the Berg and all the Brixen Valley. But he could not make such a promise. It was one thing to face her servant. It would be another thing to defeat him.

Still, he was ready to try.

"Mistress . . ." Rudi held his breath for a moment. "Do you have enough magic to make the coin sing again?"

The witch raised an eyebrow. She pulled the golden guilder from her apron pocket and pressed it between her hands, as if warming it. Then she whispered to it, so quietly that Rudi could not make out the words. Setting the coin on the small table, she sat back and folded her hands, waiting.

Then, so faint at first that Rudi could barely hear it, the music came.

The sound grew louder, and louder still, until there could be no mistake. It was the same music he'd heard that first night, when he'd brought the coin down the mountain through the snow and sleet. A tuneless song that sounded something like the wail of a pennywhistle.

Rudi's eyes grew wide, as did the witch's grin.

Then she snatched up the coin, muffling its tune.

"*Shhh!*" she hissed, and it fell silent. She tucked it again into her pocket.

But her grin did not fade. "And now, young Rudolf," she said, "you needn't try to find my rebellious servant. For *he* will come to *you*."

Rudi shivered at the thought. Then another worry came to him. "But if he does, how will we find the other children?"

"No doubt you'll think of something," said the witch, standing and stretching. "You has good instincts. When the time comes, you'll know what to do."

Rudi smiled weakly. He hoped she was right, for suddenly his mind once more felt as blank as slate.

He tried to think. "Can you still hear the search party?" For if he was going to stand outside with the singing coin and wait for her servant to find him, it would be nice to have friends in the vicinity.

She tilted her head and closed her eyes, listening. Finally, she said, "They're near enough. I expect the coin's singing will bring them to you as well."

"What about the other children?" said Rudi. "Can you hear them?"

She listened once more. Then she shook her head, and Rudi's hopes fell.

"They cannot be far," she said. "Mayhaps he is using magic to cloak their whereabouts—the nasty fiend. There's numerous caves roundabout this mountain. None as big and cozy as this one, but he may have found one large enough to hold a gaggle of children. I suspects my stolen magic is hidden in the same place. He hasn't got much imagination."

"So then." Rudi counted the steps on his nervous fingers. "I go out. He comes to find me. I offer the coin in exchange for my friends. But I can't let him have it."

The witch snapped her fingers. "A perfect plan."

Rudi wasn't so sure. "If he's as powerful as you say he is, what's to stop him from smiting me on the spot, taking the coin, and locking us all inside the mountain forever?"

She shrugged. "I suppose you'd best not get smitten."

He scowled to conceal his fear. "This is *not* a perfect plan."

"Have you forgotten already what you've learned? He cannot resist the coin, and yet he cannot abide its music. You must take advantage of his torment and indecision." She drew the golden guilder from her pocket and laid it on Rudi's palm. "This coin holds the last remnant of my magic. Without it, I am defenseless. I am truly putting my life in your hand."

Rudi gulped. "Are you sure this is a good idea?" Once more, he feared he was not equal to the task.

"You are Gussie's grandson. I can think of no

better person." She folded Rudi's fingers over the coin. "Rub it between your hands, and it will sing. Its magic will give you some measure of protection, but not much. Whatever you do, bring it back to me, or all will be lost." She patted him on the shoulder. "Best get going before the light wanes."

And so, with the golden guilder in his pocket, his father's best knife on his belt, and his heart in his throat, Rudi stepped out into the daylight.

He followed the path away from the tall crevice that marked the door to the witch's cave. It ought to be easy enough to find again, at any rate.

The coin lay quiet in his pocket for the moment. Rudi hoped he would not need it. Not yet. First he wanted to find some clue to the whereabouts of his friends.

He scrambled on the mountain for what seemed like hours, though the sun remained high. There was no sign of the other children. No bits of cloth tied to the branches by the search party. Rudi wondered if he was searching on the wrong side of the mountain. But he dared not venture too far. He could not become lost. He continued on, keeping within sight of the crevice that marked the witch's door.

Then, as he searched, Rudi became aware of a faint but steady noise: a rhythmic banging, as of rock against rock. It was not a sound an animal would make, or the wind. He followed it, keeping quiet. He slid one hand into his pocket, ready to bring out the coin. With his other hand he grasped the handle of his knife.

Rudi followed the knocking sound to an outcropping of jagged rocks half-hidden by pine saplings. Warily, he stepped closer. Then, though the sun was hot, Rudi felt a breath of cool air coming from between the rocks.

Pushing the branches aside, he found a large crack in the rock as high as he was tall, and only wide enough to push his head inside, if he'd wanted to. But he did not want to. The cool air flowed out from the crack, and so did the banging. He'd heard that sound before, but he couldn't recall when or where.

Rudi put his face to the crack. He held his breath. Then he called, "Hello?"

His voice echoed. He had found a cave.

The banging stopped. Now Rudi heard a faint rustling noise from deep inside the cave, as a creature shuffling in the dirt. Perhaps it was a badger, ready to attack.

Or the witch's servant.

The rustling grew louder. Something was coming toward him.

Rudi backed away, ready to run.

Suddenly a face appeared.

CHAPTER 26

"I KNEW you'd come, Rudi!" Susanna Louisa beamed out at him through the crack in the stone. Then she displayed the rock she held. "See? People can always hear me better when I knock with a stone."

"Is it really you?" Rudi tried to keep his voice low, but he could not contain his joy. "Are you all right? Is everyone in there with you?"

Susanna Louisa nodded. "Everybody," she whispered. "We're faring well enough, except it's cold and damp and I think it's past lunch. We found some biscuits, but they're dry as dust. There's a spring, too, with clear water, thank goodness. Can you take us home, Rudi?"

"I hope so. We need to get you out first."

"There's no way out," she said. "No way at all.

178

We've looked. We came in this way, but that nasty fiddler closed up the door, and now it's nothing but a window. I don't like that fiddler."

Rudi gulped. "He's not in there now, is he?"

"Oh, no," said Susanna Louisa. "We've not seen him since he locked us in here. I hope I never see him again."

"So do I," said Rudi, though he knew it could not be avoided. He had no doubt the fiddler was somewhere close at hand.

"Is there anything else in the cave with you?" Rudi asked her. "Any other . . . provisions?"

Susanna Louisa shrugged. "There's a whole pile of stuff, but it's mostly useless. There's a teapot, but it's cracked, and anyway there's no tea. There's a good, strong rope, but no room for skipping in here. A basket of potatoes, but nothing to cook them with." She wrinkled her nose. "Nobody likes raw potatoes."

"The witch was right," Rudi whispered. "Her magic is here too." And then, to Susanna, "What else? Is the fiddle in there?"

"Oh, yes, it's here. But that fiddler said don't touch it. He said don't make so much as a peep. And who knows? Perhaps he's watching us. We haven't touched the fiddle. We've been quiet as can be. I even knocked quietly. We don't like being stuck in here, but we don't want him mad at us neither. He's a mean one."

"I know." Rudi glanced around nervously. He turned back to Susanna Louisa with renewed urgency. "Listen to me, Susanna. All those things inside the cave—the teapot, the fiddle, the potatoes, everything—they're magic."

"The potatoes?"

Rudi nodded.

Susanna Louisa's eyes grew wide. "I'm glad we didn't eat them."

Rudi laughed, and for that he was so grateful, he could have kissed her. But he only said, "Silly girl."

"When can we go home, Rudi?"

"Don't worry," he said, trying to sound grown-up. "We'll have you home and skipping rope in no time. I'm just . . . not sure how, yet."

A satisfied grin spread across Susanna's face. "I know how! If all these things are magic, then I know how to get us out." She hummed to herself.

Rudi blinked at her. He yearned to know more, but time was short. He would have to trust her.

"Do it, then. And when you do, be sure to take everything with you from inside the cave. As much as you can carry."

"Even the fiddle?"

"Especially the fiddle. Will you tell the others?"

She nodded solemnly. "Anything for you, Rudi."

His face burned, and he cleared his throat. "Once you're all free, wait here until you hear music. And when you hear it, this is what I want you to do."

He gave quick instructions to Susanna Louisa. "Can you remember that?"

"Oh, yes," she said, nearly bouncing inside the cave.

"Good. I'm going now to try to distract the fiddler. Once you are out, remember to keep quiet until you hear the music." And with that, Rudi retraced his steps toward the witch's cave. If the witch was right, and the fiddler truly was driven by greed and vanity, his plan should work. At least, Rudi hoped it would.

After a few minutes walking, Rudi looked around once more. The witch's servant had been too quiet. Rudi suspected that Susanna Louisa was right, and they were being watched.

It was time to find out. As he hurried down the path, Rudi pulled the golden guilder from his pocket and rubbed it between his palms.

For a moment there was nothing. Rudi wondered if he was supposed to tell it something, the way the witch had done. He whispered, *"Sing!"*

And it did. The coin sang, and then it wailed, filling the air with piercing music.

Before he had gone ten steps, Rudi heard another noise behind him. An unmistakable grating growl that blew down the mountain on a chill wind and became a screeching in his ears, as if in answer to the coin's wailing.

The time had come. All would be won—or lost—in the next few moments.

Fighting the urge to drop the coin and cover his ears, Rudi ran down the path toward the witch's door, with the fiddler on his heels. He jammed the coin deep into his pocket, and was grateful to find that its song was not muffled. He hurled himself over boulders and tore through brambles.

The screeching followed him, and though it was July, the wind blew as cold as January on his neck. He plunged onward, not daring to look back.

Rudi rounded a bend. Far ahead, at the crevice's opening, was a sight that made his heart leap.

The search party.

They were milling about, rattling their weapons, such as they were. The men of Brixen were not hunters or bowmen. They were farmers and craftsmen and merchants, and they carried pitchforks and slingshots and knives.

Rudi uttered a cry of relief as he stumbled down the path toward them. Now he would have allies, and not a heartbeat too soon. Together they might yet have a chance to defeat the witch's servant.

As Rudi drew near, Marco stepped forward and held up his arm.

"Stay back, boy! This is a dangerous place!"

Rudi skidded to a halt. He wanted to tell Marco, *Of course it's dangerous! The fiddler is almost upon me! Can't you hear him?* But he was so winded from running, he could manage only "huh?"

Then, as quickly as it had started, the screeching stopped. Rudi turned. The witch's servant was gone, though the air remained as cold as winter.

Quickly, Rudi patted his pocket and said, *"Shhh!"* To his relief, the coin quieted its music, though it continued to echo faintly in his ears. Perhaps it was a phantom sound. Or perhaps the coin did not want to be forgotten.

Marco tugged Rudi closer. "We've found the witch's lair. There's a low door within that crevice. We need someone small enough to crawl inside, and you're just the one to do it. Take this." He held out an axe nearly as big as Rudi. "She's got the children in there, I'll wager. Once they're safely out, chop her into a thousand pieces."

Rudi's breath stuck in his throat. He could only shake his head.

"No matter," said Marco. "Then just flush her out, and we'll do the rest." The search party nodded and shook their fists.

"No!" Rudi gasped. "You don't understand. It's not the witch. . . ."

"I can help," came a voice from behind Rudi. "I

can help you destroy the witch."

Rudi knew that voice. As if to confirm his fears, the air grew yet colder, turning his breath to white vapor.

"You again!" said Marco. "I'd know that motley shirt anywhere." He shivered, from the sight of the man before him, or from the cold, or from both.

"Yes, it is I," said the fiddler. A gust of wind blew, and then a spray of sleet, hissing on the sunbaked earth. "How else can I make amends for taking your precious children? I am but a servant of the witch, bound to do her bidding. But have no worries, for your children are safe."

"Where are they? We want to see them now." Marco stepped forward, swinging his great axe onto his shoulder.

The fiddler inched backward. "Certainly, good sir. You shall see them straightaway. Just as soon as this young fellow pays me what is mine." He nodded toward Rudi, and his eyes gleamed. The sleet came down in sheets now, so that every man shivered and pulled up his hood.

Rudi only gulped and shook his head. Icy pellets stabbed his face. The coin lay quiet in his pocket and would stay there as long as Rudi had breath.

"What's he talking about, Rudi?" said Marco.

"It's the same payment as before," offered the fiddler. "One golden guilder. He's finally found it, good lad, and it's in his pocket. Isn't it?" He held out his hand.

Marco sighed. "Pay the man, boy, so we can get our children and go home."

The fiddler took a step closer, his face barely able to contain his triumph. Rudi recoiled. The witch's words rang in his head: *If he takes possession of this coin, all will be lost.*

"Wait!" Otto pushed his way to the front of the group. "How can we trust this servant of the witch? I say bring out our children first."

The fiddler stifled a sneer. "Very well," he said. "They are inside the cave, with the witch." He pointed beyond them to the witch's door.

The search party turned and regarded the low door once more.

This moment's distraction was enough for the fiddler. He reached out and grabbed Rudi by the collar, yanking it with brutal strength. Then, with a sly grin, he reached for Rudi's pocket, and the coin.

Suddenly, the fiddler cried out in surprise and pain. The wind and sleet ceased, and from somewhere upslope, growing louder with every heartbeat, there came a new sound.

It was the hum of a bow scraping across the strings of a fiddle.

CHAPTER 27

THE SOUND of the fiddle pierced the air, noisy and sour, like an ill-tempered cat trying to sing. The witch's servant released Rudi and covered his ears, his face twisting in anger and confusion.

But to Rudi's ears, it was the most beautiful sound he could imagine.

The children were free.

Rudi scrambled away from the man's grasp and searched his pocket. The coin was still there.

With a roar, the witch's servant started up the path in the direction of the fiddle music. "Who dares to steal my magic?"

Rudi gasped in horror. He pulled the coin from his pocket, rubbing it awake. He held it above his head, and its sound carried in all directions.

The servant stopped. He turned toward Rudi

once more, and his eyes were black with fury. "You!" he said. "Give me that coin." He stepped closer, grimacing in pain, or desire, or both.

Rudi's legs felt as if they would melt under him.

Then, from behind the witch's servant came the fiddle music once more, and Rudi saw a flash of something in the man's face.

Torment and indecision. The witch's words again: *Take advantage of his torment and indecision.*

Rudi held the coin high and slowly backed away, toward the gathering of men standing at the witch's door.

The servant growled, but he followed Rudi only a step before turning back again toward the sound of the approaching fiddle.

"You're stuck," Rudi said, though the witch's servant did not hear him. "You can't decide which magic to grab for. And it's all out of your possession now."

The sound of the fiddle grew louder. In a moment's time, the children of Brixen came around the bend, singing an old song—a song Rudi had known by heart since he was very small. He had never really thought about the words before, but he did now.

> The secret lair is cold and damp.
> Has not a blanket nor a lamp.
> Sing these words and count to three,

Sing these words and you'll be free:
'Home is where I want to be.
At my hearth with a cup of tea.'
One . . . two . . . THREE!

Behind Rudi, the search party shouted in gladness and relief to see their children marching toward them, safe and happy.

"Stop!" roared the witch's servant. "Bring those things to me. They are mine!" He stomped in fury, but Rudi noticed that the icy air had softened to a cool mountain breeze.

Rudi held out the singing coin, which for a moment seemed to hold the witch's servant transfixed.

Upon seeing this, Rudi's friends hurried past, keeping a wary eye on the witch's servant. Nicolas, the boastful boy, tromped past lugging a basket of potatoes. Clara and Petra scurried by with a cracked teapot and a coil of rope. Konrad shepherded young Roger past the servant, who stood in an agony of indecision. Marta carried one of the babies, who buried his face in his sister's neck. Every child carried some piece of the witch's bounty. Even the smallest infant clutched a potato in his tiny hands. They were ordinary objects such as could be found in any kitchen in Brixen. But Rudi knew they were much more than that.

At the rear marched Susanna Louisa, with the

188

fiddle planted under her chin and the bow nearly as long as she was tall, making a noise that drowned out everything, even the wailing of the coin. Rudi quickly closed his fist around it.

The witch's servant shook himself as if he'd been slapped. A wicked grin spread across his face as he turned toward Susanna Louisa and stepped into the center of the path, blocking her way. "Come here, my dear, and I'll show you how to play that fiddle," he called, in a voice as thick as cream.

Susanna Louisa stuttered to a halt with one last screeching, echoing scrape of bow across strings. "Rudi?" she squeaked in the shuddering silence. "Now what?"

Rudi had no time to think. The servant stood between him and Susanna Louisa, barely more than an arm's length from each of them. One lunge in either direction and he would have the fiddle, or the coin. Rudi did not want to find out what might happen if the servant had either piece of magic in his possession.

With a quick rub to set it singing once more, Rudi held the coin higher, praying he'd be quick enough to keep it away from the evil snatching hand.

Now the servant turned his back on Susanna and faced Rudi, who allowed himself a glimmer of satisfaction. With his free hand, he gave a small wave. Susanna Louisa noticed.

But the servant did not. He had eyes only for the singing coin.

"Foolish boy," he spat. "That coin is nothing but trouble for you. Give it to me and I will silence that wretched noise."

Rudi shook his head and stepped back. Momentarily forgotten, Susanna Louisa scurried past them both, to the waiting arms of the search party.

The servant grinned at Rudi, yet his eyes flared in anger. "Why do you meddle in business that's between me and the old woman?" He took a step closer.

"The Brixen Witch's business *is* my business," answered Rudi, standing his ground. "And theirs." He nodded toward the search party, who were celebrating a joyful reunion with their children. "They may not know it, but they need their witch."

The servant gave an evil laugh. "They care nothing for the witch. They're ready to chop her into a thousand pieces."

Rudi shook his head slowly. "Not since you proved yourself to be a liar. Now they know the children were not in the witch's cave as you told them they were."

"Why do you resist me? The witch's time is past. When I rule this mountain, you will forget there ever was a witch."

Rudi squinted at him. "What will you do about a stillborn calf when you rule this mountain?"

The witch's servant wrinkled his nose. "Don't be absurd, boy. You think I would bother with the tiny details of your little farming life?"

"What about elderberry tarts? Do you like elderberry tarts?"

"Give me that coin, boy, or I'll take it from you!"

"Do it, then," said Rudi, for now he was angry too.

But the witch's servant hesitated. His eyes flickered to the scene behind Rudi, and he hissed with foul breath.

Just steps away, the search party stood, weapons at hand. Each man had his free arm around a cluster of children. Each child still held a bit of the witch's magic. And in the midst of the children and their fathers, with hands on hips and a defiant look in her eye, stood a tiny old woman.

Rudi turned back to face the servant. "It seems you're outnumbered."

The man bared his sharp teeth and growled in anger. He lunged for the golden guilder in Rudi's hand.

This time, Rudi was ready. He dodged out of reach and tossed the coin high over his shoulder.

As it rose, it wailed more sharply than ever. Then, just as the coin reached its apex, the ragged notes seemed to rearrange themselves in the air. As it fell, the coin played a song so pure and clear, Rudi was certain the nightingale would hide in shame. The coin landed in the witch's outstretched hand, and a breath of wind blew, warm and full of the scent of summer.

The witch's magic had been returned to her. All of it.

The servant's eyes grew wide, and his face grew pale. Then, having no weapon and no other choice, he turned and fled.

"No need to worry," announced the tiny old woman, dropping the coin into her apron pocket. "He'll not bother you anymore."

CHAPTER 28

SNOW FELL upon Brixen.

It began before dawn and continued throughout the day. It brushed against the windowpanes, piling up, inch upon inch, until the entire landscape was muffled in a cloak of silvery white.

The children hurried to finish their lessons and their chores, then bundled into boots and heavy woolens. They disappeared into barns and sheds, emerging with their sleds and their skis. The grass would not be seen again until spring, and soon the excitement of new snow would wear thin, but the first snowfall was always a cause for celebration.

And thus began another long winter in Brixen.

It had been months since the children had returned to a joyous celebration that lasted for days, with feasting and dancing and the ringing of bells. Still, every parent's heart lurched at the memory of the time when they were gone, and no child argued when admonished to stay close to home.

Stories were told in Brixen that winter, during the long, dark nights, of frightful witches and silver spoons and magic potatoes and cursed coins.

Susanna Louisa told of how a simple rope-skipping song was really a magic incantation that released the children from their rocky prison.

"It helps if you throw magic potatoes at the crack when you sing *one ... two ... THREE,*" she added, and then she was sent to bed.

Marco the blacksmith told of how the search party came upon a frail old woman wandering the mountain, probably a lost traveler from Petz. Just in time, they'd steered her away from the witch's door, admonishing her to leave the coin, which surely had a hex upon it. She'd thanked them for their advice, and for the collection of humble items the children gave her, which they had found in a nearby cave.

"I suppose they belonged to the witch and her servant," said Marco. "But they can spare a few things for a poor old woman. Funny thing, though—the witch never showed herself, the fearsome creature."

Otto the baker told of how Rudi chased off the witch's servant, and good riddance.

"I hear tell the witch punished her servant for allowing the children to escape. He's locked in a cave high on the Berg, closed up inside the rock. You can hear him screaming during the fiercest storms, and anyone who wanders close enough can feel his icy breath blowing out from the cracks in the rock."

But of course they were only stories, and stories are meant to be told and embellished, until they become folktale and legend.

Though they looked at him sidelong and whispered behind his back, no one dared ask Rudi to tell his stories. He would not have told them anyway, though Rudi had stories that only he could tell. After all, he had been on the mountain alone. He had found the children in their cave. He had placed himself between all his friends and the witch's servant. Some folk said that Rudi had met the Brixen Witch herself and that she had shared with him some of her secrets.

The witch had also given Rudi something else.

"Do you think I'll ever learn to play this thing?" he asked one night.

"I surely do hope so," said his father, covering his ears and clenching his pipe between his teeth. "You're worrying the cows with that noise, even from here."

"Give it time," said his mother, pouring tea and passing the elderberry tarts. "But perhaps it would be best to wait until summertime, when you can practice outdoors?"

Oma rocked forward in her chair. "Why are you having so much trouble?" she whispered. "I thought that was a magic fiddle."

Rudi shook his head. "I think she kept that part for herself. Besides," and he shook the bow at her, "you know it's bad luck to talk of such things."

THE
DRAGON
C H R O N I C L E S

"I loved each one of Susan Fletcher's dragon books.
She makes the dragons as real as the people."—JANE YOLEN

"An intricate blend of humor, adventure, and sadness. . . .
A satisfying fantasy set in a world that could be yesterday—or tomorrow."
—*VOYA* on *Dragon's Milk*

"Readers empathize with the deftly crafted characters, always aware
of the struggle between good and evil, honor and dishonor. . . . Fletcher pens
some of the best yarns around."—*Booklist* on *Flight of the Dragon Kyn*

"An absorbing fantasy."—*Horn Book Magazine* on *Sign of the Dove*

Atheneum

EBOOK EDITIONS ALSO AVAILABLE
From Atheneum Books for Young Readers][KIDS.SimonandSchuster.com

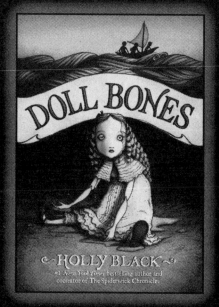

Unlock the magic within.

Holly doesn't think of herself as
special until the day she opens a
pathway to a treacherous world
where she is powerful. Magical.

And where she is considered
to be a threat so dangerous.
the royals want her *dead*.

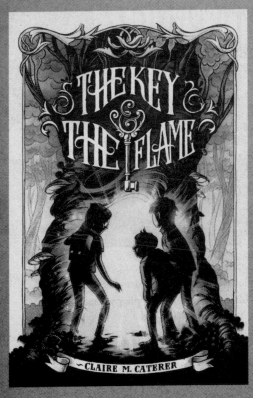